MERRY'S WORLD
Jamestown in 1621

The glasshouse

The glasshouse

James River

Jamestown

Jamestown

SHADOWS IN THE GLASSHOUSE

by
Megan McDonald

Printed in the United States of America.
00 01 02 03 04 05 RRD 10 9 8 7 6 5 4 3 2 1

History Mysteries® and American Girl®
are trademarks of Pleasant Company.

PERMISSIONS & PICTURE CREDITS
The following individuals and organizations have generously given permission to reprint
illustrations contained in "A Peek into the Past": p. 125—©Bettmann/CORBIS ("The New Life"
broadside); p. 126—State Capitol, Commonwealth of Virginia, Courtesy The Library of Virginia
(English ships); p. 128—©Bettmann/CORBIS ("The Starving Time"); p. 129—©Bettmann/COR-
BIS (three field hands); Rare Books Division, The New York Public Library, Astor, Lenox and
Tilden Foundations (ship company broadside); Colonial Williamsburg Foundation (tobacco label);
p. 130—"Arrival of the Maids" by Sidney E. King, used with permission; Arte & Immagini srl/
CORBIS (vase); p. 131—Photograph by Robert Llewellyn (glassblower).

Cover and Map Illustrations: Paul Bachem
Line Art: Laszlo Kubinyi
Editorial Direction: Jodi Evert
Art Direction: Lynne Wells
Design: Laura Moberly and Justin Packard

Library of Congress Cataloging-in-Publication Data

McDonald, Megan.
Shadows in the glasshouse / by Megan McDonald. — 1st ed.
p. cm. — (History mysteries)
"American girl."
Summary: While working as an indentured servant for a Jamestown glassmaker
in 1621, twelve-year-old Merry uncovers a case of sabotage.

ISBN 1-58485-093-0 — ISBN 1-58485-092-2 (pbk.)
1. Jamestown (Va.)—History—Juvenile fiction. 2. Virginia—History—Colonial period, ca. 1600-
1775—Juvenile fiction. [1. Jamestown (Va.)—History—Fiction. 2. Virginia—History—Colonial
period, ca. 1600-1775—Fiction. 3. Glass manufacture—Fiction. 4. Indentured servants—
Fiction. 5. Orphans—Fiction. 6. Mystery and detective stories.] I. Title. II. Series.
PZ7.M478419 Sh 2000   [Fic]—dc21   00-029336

For Richard

TABLE OF CONTENTS

CHAPTER I
THE FLYING HART

Twelve-year-old Meredith Shipman carved out a corner for herself among the ribs and ropes of the cramped, narrow 'tween deck, the low-ceilinged space between the ship's deck above and the hold below. She could barely make out the ship's skeleton in the dark. *I cannot imagine it any darker inside the belly of a whale,* she thought.

Her thin, moth-eaten blanket was so damp it gave her little comfort. She covered her nose so she wouldn't have to smell the musty wet wool. The rough edges of the wooden planking dug into her back as she tried to find a comfortable position.

Her legs and arms were folded tightly, like a quilt inside an overpacked chest. Merry yearned to stretch her limbs, no longer spending most of her time bent and cramped. She tugged on her sleeves, trying to pull them over her wrists for warmth. It was no use. Her sleeves had grown too short during three long months at sea.

Why on earth do they call this ship the Flying Hart, *when it scarcely seems to crawl its way to the New World?* she wondered.

She and other orphans and servants had been confined to a corner of the 'tween deck most of the journey. They were crowded together at the far end of the ship's stern, no better than the pigs, chickens, and goats on board.

Three months felt like forever. Forever since she'd known ground beneath her feet that did not shift and sway. Forever since she'd had a drink of water that was not black and full of worms. Forever since she'd combed her hair, now tangled and matted as a bird's nest.

"We'll all die o' the fever. If'n not, them wild beasties'll getcha," whispered a boy called Fitch. "Deadly claws and six-inch fangs. One man had his leg bit off, I heard. By a giant crab. Climbed right out of the James River, it did. And if it aren't the wild beasts, it'll sure be poison arrows."

"Them's just stories," said a girl by the name of Lottie.

"Are not," said Fitch. "Ask any o' them on the crew. They'll tell ye."

Merry hoped Lottie was right.

Lottie continued. "Like I've been telling you, they'll work us sunup to sundown, they will. For not so much as a farthing. If ye get caught clacking your tongue, they whip ye with a knotted rope. If ye try to run away, they'll tie ye to a tree."

Merry shivered. She tried to block out the stories, but

she couldn't help listening to every whispered rumor. Each one left the bitter taste of fear in her mouth. True, she'd soon become an indentured servant like the others. Bound for the New World, they had told her. Jamestown, Virginia. *Names. That's all they are,* Merry thought.

Indentured servant. The dreadful words stuck in Merry's mind, lodged there like a splinter from the ship's deck. An indentured servant was little more than a slave, as far as she could tell. Turning toward the wall, Merry curled on her side and hugged her knees tight against her.

Another boy said, "I heard they make you sleep in a dung-filled cow barn. Or a chicken coop. I knew a girl in London—her own father sold her to a farmer for the price of a handkerchief."

Merry wished she could shut out the stories, but the 'tween deck was so crammed and crowded, there was no getting away from the others. She pulled the blanket over her head. Little good it did. The rise and fall of voices, mixed with the mewing of the ship's cat, kept her from sleep.

Merry felt something scurry across her leg in the darkness. She bolted upright. A rat!

It was no use trying to sleep. She looked around at the faces of her shipmates. They hovered in the darkness like pale ghosts. Merry reached into her pocket and pulled out the hardtack she'd saved from supper. Chewing the biscuit was work, and gave her something to do, until she realized that she'd bitten into a maggot. A month ago she would have spat it out, but tonight she was so hungry she closed her eyes and swallowed.

"There'll be no cow barns or chicken coops for me," claimed an orphan named Alexander Purdee. "I signed a contract of me own free will puttin' meself in service to Thomas Nicholson the blacksmith for seven years to learn his trade. He'll not be treatin' *me* like some animal."

Fine for him, thought Merry. *He's chosen to come here. And he's a boy. Boys can learn a trade.*

"No matter," said the other boy. "I knew a lad who signed up, too, and he soon sent word back to England beggin' his mum to send him food and pleadin' to get back home."

"People starve in Jamestown," said another.

"Can't be no worse than this ship, then," said Fitch. "We've been down to nothin' but maggoty biscuits for weeks." He began to sing, imitating the sailors:

We ate the mice, we ate the rats,
And through the hold we ran like cats.

Even after the stories died down, Merry could not sleep. What she feared most—more than hunger, more than a cruel master, more than wild beasts lurking in the forests—was never seeing her older sister again. Years ago, Merry had lived through the death of her parents. She couldn't bear the thought of losing Margaret, too. Merry whispered her sister's name over and over, like a sleep chant, as she fingered the blue glass beads she always wore around her neck. She and Margaret each had a strand— the only gift they had left from their parents.

Margaret was the only person Merry had in the world. She was still back in London, working at the Sign of the Swan tavern as a kitchen maid. It had been three months since Merry had seen the rooftops of London disappear into the fog. Three months since she'd been taken from her sister. Merry's eyes smarted just thinking of it.

She and Margaret had lived on the money Margaret earned for her work in the tavern kitchen. The owners had given them a pallet to sleep on in the storeroom. Usually Margaret brought her the tavern's leftover bread or hard rolls, sometimes even a cake or a crumpet.

Merry closed her eyes and tried to find a picture of her old life, before she and Margaret were orphaned. She remembered when she was nearly six, growing up in a real house with real beds to sleep on and a garden full of roses. Roses with names like Black Beauty and Bonfire Night. She had lain awake many a night in the dark next to Margaret, while they recited the names of roses. Her sister had put the names to a tune, making them into a lullaby just for Merry. But the thing she remembered best was waking every morning to a steaming bowl of porridge that her mother set before her.

After their parents died, Merry and Margaret had lived at the edge of hunger, but they survived. They had kept themselves fed one way or another, even if only with crusts of bread picked up from the streets when Margaret ran out of coins. Merry was not about to let stories of wild animals and poison arrows get the better of her.

⚡

The next morning, Merry opened her eyes and tried to breathe through her mouth so she would not have to take in the smell. Another night of seasickness and Fitch not being able to keep down the maggoty biscuits. The only light in the dark recesses of the 'tween deck came through the main hatch. A smaller, grated hatch just above Merry let in slivers of gray light. Merry stared up through the grate, trying to glimpse a patch of sky, but all she could see was the rushing back and forth of the crew's feet.

It seemed hours before she was allowed on deck that day. Merry climbed the ladder from her dark corner and stepped out into the open air. Since she'd been forced aboard this ship, she'd only been let out once a day for a walk around the deck.

Merry took great gulps of fresh, sweet air. She memorized the warm fingers of early October sunshine on her cheeks, the press of it on her closed lids. For later. For the long hours when she smelled only the stench of chamber pots, stagnant water, and bodies crowded too close, a stench stronger than the garbage-filled gutters of London.

Merry leaned out over the ship's rail, closed her eyes, and took in another deep breath.

Eight-year-old Thomas Norton ran down from the side rail just opposite the main mast. Merry knew that he was traveling with his mother to Jamestown, where his wealthy father had set up a glassmaking business. There were no other children his age among the paying passengers aboard the *Flying Hart*, so Thomas sometimes slipped away to talk with the servant children, especially Merry.

"Merry, Merry, have you heard? I had to come tell you. Mother says we're close now. I almost think I see land."

Merry laughed. "Oh, you do, do you?" Not in all her twelve years had she wanted anything as much as she wanted to set foot on land.

"At last I'll see my father!" said Thomas. "He was too ill to come for us. Will you join your family in Jamestown, too?" asked Thomas.

"No," said Merry. "I haven't a mother and father like you do. And my sister's still in England."

"Why are you here, then?" asked Thomas.

"I am on an adventure." Merry tried her best to think of it that way. Pretending it was an adventure gave her strength.

"Are you treasure hunting?"

"Not that kind of adventure, Thomas," said Merry.

"Tell me what kind!" Thomas begged.

"I'm not really sure, to be honest." Merry sighed. "If only I had not been chasing pigeons that day down by the wharves in London. I made it a game, really. I raced the pigeons for crusts of bread the vendors left behind, and the pigeons flapped their wings in a great flurry. That's when the captain's men saw me and took me."

"They took you?" asked Thomas.

Merry could not keep the anger from her voice. "I was kidnapped. A burly man offered me a meat pie, and I was so hungry I took it. Next thing I knew he grabbed me and forced me into a room where I could see nothing but smoke from men's pipes." Merry shuddered, remembering the strong hands that dug into her arms like claws. She screamed and flailed, kicked and bit her captors as they dragged her down to a shanty by the docks. There they gagged her and tied her up until nightfall, when they smuggled her aboard ship under the cover of darkness.

"Were you scared?"

"It was terribly dark that night, and I could scarcely make out shadows. I must have hit my head because next thing I knew, I woke up on the bare, cold floor below deck. The dungeon, I called it, when I first set eyes on the place."

"Are you a murderer?" Thomas asked. "I've heard they send murderers to Jamestown. And jailbirds and thieves."

"And orphans," said Merry. "They need anybody who can work."

"But they shouldn't have kidnapped you," said Thomas. "That's not fair!" Just then, Mistress Norton called to Thomas from the hatchway. He scrambled across the tangles of line and down the steep ladder. Merry watched Mistress Norton's beaver-skin hat disappear slowly down the ladder to the 'tween deck.

Well-to-do passengers like the Nortons slept below, too, but they stayed in the middle section of the 'tween deck, near the hatchway for fresh air. The ceiling was highest there, and they had room to stand up straight and move around. There were no real walls, just sheets hung to give those passengers some privacy. Merry shielded her eyes and peered down the hatchway, where she could see Thomas hiding and scampering among the sheets.

But she could not bear to go below yet. Just a few more breaths of clean air.

Merry gazed into the dark, murky water below, as if it held her fortune.

"Better take care that you not fall in, miss." She turned to see her friend Angelo, who was smiling at her with a gleam in his brown eyes. Angelo was a few years older than Merry, and she'd come to know that older-brother, teasing look of his in the long weeks and months at sea.

They'd met early in the journey, one day when Merry's cord of beads had broken and scattered across the deck. Merry and Angelo had chased after the precious beads like children in a game of marbles. Some of them had been lost to the sea, and Merry had struggled not to give in to tears.

The words "thank you" stuck in her throat, but Angelo knew just what to say. He told her he was a glassmaker's apprentice, and as soon as he learned the art of making colored glass, he'd be sure to make Merry some new glass beads to replace the ones she'd lost. Ever since then, he'd watched out for her during the journey. He was the only person on board who'd shown her such kindness.

"You do not seem as merry as your name suggests," Angelo said to her now, his Italian accent rising and falling like a ship on waves.

Merry sighed. "We're nearing land, Angelo."

"You're not happy? You want to stay on this miserable ship forever?"

" 'Tis not that," said Merry. "I know nothing about this Jamestown. I've heard such stories I know not what to believe. At least you have a place to go, and work you care about."

"I knew not what to expect when they smuggled me out of Italy, along with Bernardo, the master, and four other glassblowers," said Angelo. "But I keep inside my heart two friends, *speranza e fortuna*—hope and luck. They help me trust that good things will come."

Merry bristled at the mention of Bernardo. The day Merry's beads scattered across the deck, he had stood there laughing and hadn't moved to help.

Angelo reached into his pocket and brought out his

well-worn copy of *The Art of Glass,* by Antonio Neri. Merry had seen him scribbling in it countless times. The margins were filled with notes and formulas.

"See here? Soon I hope to be making more than beads. Clear glass!" said Angelo. "Think of it. In Italy, we already make *cristallo*—glass clear as water. *Trasparente.* But the formula is a secret."

"A secret?"

"Only Italian glassblowers know how to make *cristallo.* That's why we were smuggled out of Italy. Captain Norton, young Thomas's father, hoped that we might make the formula work in England. It didn't work there, but he has high hopes for glassmaking in the New World. We'll have all the supplies we need, if the stories are true."

"What does the New World have that England lacks?"

"In England, there wasn't enough wood to fire the furnaces we need to make glass. But in the New World, there are forests as wide as this ocean! Master Webbe, who runs the glasshouse for Captain Norton, hopes to make great profits. And I want to become an artisan, a master glassmaker!"

How Merry longed to know her own future, as Angelo did. Just then, the ship rose up, and Merry clutched her stomach. She let out a long, slow breath, as she'd taught herself to do to ward off seasickness.

"Storm's blowing in," said Angelo. Merry could feel her stomach lurch at the thought.

"I'm afraid our troubles at sea have not yet finished. God help us," said Angelo.

"'Tis the time of year for ill winds," Merry said. She shuddered as she remembered the shrieking winds and raging waters that had caused the ship to take on water just days ago. There was nothing worse than being huddled in her tiny dark corner with water seeping in through the cracks and dripping down from the ceiling. If the ship went down, she'd be trapped in the back of the 'tween deck with no chance for escape. She'd be left to drown, just like a ship's rat.

CHAPTER 2

ILL WINDS

Crosswinds and fierce waters raged for a day and a night and yet another day. Waves pounded the ship, sweeping over the bow, flooding the deck and forcing passengers to stay below. The ship lurched, nearly tipping on its side.

People and pallets, barrels and chests were thrown about helter-skelter. It felt as if the *Flying Hart* was spinning in circles, being tossed about aimlessly by the contrary winds, maybe even being blown farther out to sea. Fights broke out among the passengers, and Bernardo always seemed to be in the thick of them. Some passengers prayed, "Oh God, if only I had a fresh drop of water," and the sick cried out to be saved, "Oh that I was home again!"

Then there were the agonizing screams of a woman who had a baby right there on a pallet in the 'tween deck. The baby died at birth, born blue in the face, Merry

heard. She could not believe her eyes when they wrapped
the infant in sailcloth, said a prayer, and gently slipped it
through a porthole into the sea.

Merry stayed huddled in the 'tween deck, unable to
tell night from day. She listened to wind thrum through
the rigging, and waves crash against the ship. She watched
water seep in through the cracks between the boards. She
covered her nose against the strong smell of pitch and tar
the crew used to patch the cracks.

Just when Merry thought she could not stand it one
second longer, someone opened the hatch from above to
let in some air. Climbing topside, Merry gulped in air that
had no stench. A gust of wind made her skirt flap like a
sail, nearly lifting her off the deck.

"Merí! Stay below!" yelled Angelo through the roaring
wind. He was soaked through, rounding up those who'd
tried to go on deck.

In the instant he turned his back to the sea to warn
her, the ship pitched. She saw a giant wave reach up, like
the hand of a sea monster, and snatch her friend right
from the deck.

In the blink of an eye, Angelo was gone.

"Angelo!" screamed Merry into the wind. She slid
across the slick deck, rushing to look over the rail, wind
stinging her cheeks and rain battering her hair.

"Get back, you," yelled Bernardo, pushing Merry away
from the rail.

But she refused to listen to him. Merry grasped the rail to steady her sliding feet and searched the roiling sea. "He's there!" she pointed. "There! I saw him!" Angelo struggled to the surface for a few seconds before the sea swallowed him again.

"He's caught hold of the topsail halyard!" shouted Bernardo. "Hang on!" he called to Angelo.

Bernardo and several men grabbed the end of the rope that hung over the ship's side. Merry helped them pull with all her might, but the rope just slipped through her fingers, burning her hands, and the sting of salt water blinded her eyes.

At last, they hauled Angelo to the brim of the water.

He was tangled in the rope, limp as seaweed. Merry could not tell if her friend was alive.

The next thing Merry knew, Bernardo had grabbed a boat hook and snagged Angelo under the arms, raising him little by little to the ship's deck, in the same way she had seen dangling cargo loaded onto the boat. Angelo collapsed in a heap on the deck. His lips had taken on a bluish cast from the icy water, and he was shaking.

"Angelo!" cried Merry. Many hands reached to help carry him below. The men pulled out a straw pallet, set him on his side, and covered him with blankets. Angelo sputtered and coughed, but he would not open his eyes.

"He's surely had some water in his lungs," said Cook, "but he'll be fine, with some rest. Let's give him room.

Let him have his sleep now. When he wakes, I'll see that he gets a warm broth."

"You heard Cook," Bernardo said to Merry in a mean voice. "Go away! Make space for this poor soul."

Merry turned to go, stepping over pallets and around barrels. She was so upset and angry she felt as if she were choking. She climbed the ladder and stuck her head through the hatch. Even though she knew no one was allowed topside, Merry could not help climbing on deck. She tried to calm her racing heart. The winds had died a bit, but they still carried the sounds of Merry's angry voice as she shouted at wind and water, shouted back at the storm that nearly took Angelo's life.

❧

Over the next few days, Merry visited Angelo as often as she could manage to squeeze across the crowded 'tween deck, now littered with overturned barrels and chests, and ropes, hammocks, and gear that had broken loose in the storm. There had hardly been room to turn around before, and now there was nowhere to step.

Cook forced Angelo to drink a cordial of water distilled from bitter herbs. It smelled worse than rotted fish.

"If I'd known this would be the cure, I might have stayed in the sea," Angelo joked with Cook. Then, turning to Merry, he said, "'Tis because of your sharp eyes and the grace of God that I will set eyes on the New World after all. I say thanks to you, Merí."

"Aren't you forgetting something?" said a voice from beside them. Bernardo! Merry stiffened. How long had he been lurking there?

" 'Twas I who came to your rescue, no?"

"And nearly sliced my back in two with a boat hook," said Angelo. "But I am grateful nonetheless."

"Rest assured that no harm will come to you while I'm around," said Bernardo. "I need you in one piece, boy, if I hope to get any work out of you at the glasshouse."

"I am not a boy!" protested Angelo. "I'm fifteen."

"Never mind that," said Bernardo. "I'm reminding you, Angelo Lupo, you are not only to be in my service at the glasshouse. You are now indebted to me for your very life!" His eyes grew wide and he puffed himself up. Merry thought he looked quite like a dead fish.

Merry could no longer contain herself. "You! You're just a . . . a . . . bull in men's clothing," she stammered.

"And from what I've heard," scoffed Bernardo, "you are nothing but a pigeon girl with a tongue too long."

Just then came a loud call from the crow's nest. "Land, ho, Virginia!"

Passengers began scrambling to get on deck. Angelo was still too weak to move.

"I'll tell you everything I see," Merry assured Angelo. She squeezed past Bernardo and climbed up the ladder.

She smelled land before she saw it. There was something on the wind besides the familiar sting of salt air—
something that called to mind the earthworms in her
childhood garden. Pine and grass, mud and wet leaves.

Merry let the air fill her lungs, and a picture of land
fill her mind's eye. Hills and hummocks, fields and forests,
green grass. She thought there must be nothing so wonderful as to feel solid ground under her feet again.

Merry squinted, trying to make out a shape in the
distance. She thought she saw a thin black line sketched
between sea and sky. Or had she merely imagined it?

She ran to the side rail and pulled herself up to gain a
better view. As surely as her name was Meredith Shipman,
she spotted a hazy smudge on the horizon, more solid
than shadow. She was certain of it.

A thrill ran through her, a tingling, as if she could feel
the blood rushing through her veins.

Merry caught a snatch of conversation upwind from
where she stood. A craggy man with a jagged, lightning-bolt
scar down one side of his face was saying to Bernardo, "It
won't be long now. We'll be making riches in no time."

Was that all the man could think of at such a moment?
A friend of Bernardo's was no friend of hers. Besides, just
to look at the man's face gave her the shivers.

CHAPTER 3

SOLD!

At last, the hazy black line that Merry had fixed her eyes on from a distance had become a real shore, with a sandy beach, grassy banks, and tall, pointed pines that tipped their hats to the sky. As the ship left the ocean and sailed up the James River, passengers craned their necks to peer over the side rail, shouted thanks and praised God and wept for joy.

When the ship had at last dropped anchor along the shores of Jamestown, Merry saw a huddle of people on the riverbank. A scruffy dog ran to and fro, barking excitedly.

Merry felt just like that mangy little dog. Any moment now she would stretch her legs and run again! But nearly as soon as she had the thought, the shipmaster bellowed a command for all to hear. "Those of you who've not had your passage paid for," he said, "will not go ashore." A buzz of protest surged through the crowd. As the paying passengers departed, Merry was rounded up with the other servants, orphans, and prisoners. They were shoved and herded onto the foredeck like sheep in a fold.

As Merry stumbled along the foredeck, she tried frantically to look for Angelo. Try as she might, she could not catch sight of his wavy brown mop amid all the other heads rushing down the gangplank. How would she find him again?

Merry and her companions were told to line up in a row. Merry felt something as heavy as stones in the pit of her stomach. Cold, iron dread. This was the moment she had been fearing.

Merry looked up and down the row at the sorry sight they made, ragged and bedraggled. The shipmaster paced back and forth, pushing hair back from their faces and pinching their cheeks to add color. When he got to Merry, he tugged on her sleeves and told her to straighten her apron—a hopeless endeavor, as it hung in tatters.

Merry stood on tiptoe, straining for a glimpse of Angelo. She caught sight of the Nortons onshore. A tall man lifted Thomas up off the ground and hugged him, then stood listening as Mistress Norton waved her hands excitedly. *Thomas's father,* Merry thought.

Captain Norton seemed to know the scar-faced man, for Merry saw Captain Norton pull the man aside and speak to him, in between fits of coughing. Then the scar-faced man climbed back aboard the ship, along with others who'd been waiting on the shore.

The strangers approached Merry and the others in line, eyeing them up and down as if they were meat hanging at the market. Merry thought it quite rude and could hardly resist the urge to stick out her tongue at the ill-mannered man and pop-eyed woman who were sizing her up.

So much confusion! Merry heard names being called out by the shipmaster and saw him scratch marks in the ledger. One by one, people were then dragged off the ship.

"Meredith Shipman. Sold. Eighty pounds of tobacco for five years' service. Paid in full by Captain Thomas Norton," shouted the shipmaster.

At that moment, the truth struck Merry as sharply as if she had been slapped. She knew indentured servanthood meant she'd have to sign a contract and work hard. But she had been *sold*—bought and sold like a pig on market day.

And for what price? A few pounds of tobacco. She had been sold for no more than a stinking, filthy weed! Merry was so mad she thought she might boil, despite the damp October chill.

Merry told herself it was going to be all right. The ship's captain made her sign her initial—four strokes for the letter M—on a contract that he didn't even read to her.

From the back of the crowd stepped the scar-faced man. Up close, Merry noticed he was missing several of his teeth. The gaps appeared to be plugged with cork. "I'm Master Webbe, and you might be getting used to it. Come away with you, then," he said, roughly steering her through the confusion and down the gangplank.

Master Webbe? *This* was the man who ran Captain Norton's glasshouse? Was he taking her to the Nortons? That would be fine with her. But then where had Thomas gone, and the pleasant Mistress Norton? Had she spoken on Merry's behalf?

Merry teetered down the gangplank. When her feet touched ground, she could scarcely stand. Her knees buckled, it had been so long since her legs met land.

Merry stopped a moment to take in her surroundings. This New World was far worse than she had imagined. The air was thick with the stench of a pigsty. *Hardly better than the belowdecks of the ship,* Merry thought as she turned up her nose.

A cloud darkened the already gray sky above her. When Merry gazed upward, she realized the dark shape was a great flock of large wild fowl flying overhead.

Master Webbe turned to Merry and, as if just speaking to her were an effort, snarled, "Captain Norton has paid for your passage in exchange for your work at the glasshouse. No more lolling aboard ship for you. You're indentured now, under a contract of five years. You'll be working hard from sunup to sundown six days a week."

Merry could not imagine staying here, living in this wild place, working her fingers to the bone for five long years, until she found herself an old maid of seventeen!

"There'll be no running off, mind you," he continued.

"There's nowhere to go here but the forest, where wild animals'll get you. If not Indians."

Master Webbe dragged her along. If ever there was a time to pray, it was now. But in the heat of her anger, all the prayers she had ever known flew from her mind like birds from a cage. Where was he taking her? And why this Master Webbe, of all people?

Merry was suddenly splashed by a passing cart full of barrels, heading for the dock. She did not mean to stare, but the man pulling the cart had skin as black as currants.

"Hurry your step," said Master Webbe. "I've no use for a lazy wench. 'Tis work you're here for."

What will happen to me? The question rang over and over in Merry's mind.

It was an effort to steady herself on her still-wobbly legs. A tree root in the path sent Merry flying. "Clumsy girl! Pick up your feet," Master Webbe said. Merry determined to do as she was told, for the present.

Mayhap I shall run away. How hard could it be to jump a ship back to England? Merry shut out thoughts of wild animals and Indians.

When she was not concentrating on where to set her feet, Merry looked around. She saw nothing but a crude fort in the wilderness, a triangle-shaped enclosure built of split posts. It seemed no better than a camp. There were no shops and busy streets, like London. And despite all the talk she'd heard aboard ship of a glasshouse, there were certainly no houses built of glass here!

As they entered the fort, Merry noticed a homely church, a leaning storehouse, and rows of flimsy wooden shanties that had pointed roofs covered with sedge and earth. Weeds sprang from the rooftops.

Where were the alleys and streets filled with the hustle-bustle of shopkeepers and seamen, singers and fortune-tellers? Merry was instantly homesick for the drifting smell of bread baking and the familiar sound of children playing in the streets, pub-goers laughing, and hawkers calling out their wares. *This must be as far from London as one can get,* she thought miserably.

She had to dodge out of the way as a rolling ball nearly knocked her over. Grown men were bowling in the streets! Crowds were gathered in the public square, jeering and throwing garbage at a man locked in the stocks. *Splat!* Merry was hit with pig slops, which oozed down the side of her dress.

They left the fort through a wooden gate at the far corner of the enclosure and walked along a rutted path that could not even be called a road. *How can they call this place the New World? There is nothing new about it,* Merry thought. She sank up to her ankles in mud, just like the pigs that roamed the streets. How she wished for cobbles under her feet.

When it seemed Merry could no longer take another step, they reached a house—a rude hut made of wood and mud, not much larger than the henhouse that sat behind it. Master Webbe shoved her through the door into a small, dim room. Merry made out a lopsided bed, a rough wooden table and two benches by the hearth, several chests, and a few low stools.

Master Webbe left her alone, disappearing through a door that led out back. Putrid, sour smells wafted from the iron cooking pot over the hearth. Merry hoped that wasn't the smell of dinner cooking. She looked at the sorry bed and wondered if she would sleep here. Surely such a sty as this could not be where the Nortons lived?

A few minutes later, in walked a woman who intro-duced herself as Mistress Elizabeth Webbe. The woman had watery eyes, a pointed face that appeared to be mostly chin, and wisps of hair that dripped down from beneath her cap. Mistress Webbe looked Merry over as if she were a piece of half-rotted fruit.

"She looks sturdy enough," said the woman. "But I fail to see why you've brought her here. If she's to be the glasshouse girl, that's Captain Norton's business."

Glasshouse girl! Merry thought excitedly. She might get to work with Angelo.

"But Norton is ill," said Master Webbe. "Besides, he hasn't any room, with his family here now."

"So we're stuck with the girl? That's a fine mess."

And I'm stuck here, Merry thought. *With strangers who no more want to take me in than they do a stray cat.*

"I've nearly just found out myself," Master Webbe groused. "These were Norton's instructions, and I know not how I can cross him."

Mistress Webbe frowned with disapproval. "It appears you'll be staying here for the time being," she told Merry. "Master Webbe and I will be returning to England, I daresay, just as soon as Captain Norton is well. Glory be the day when I've seen the last of this wretched place!"

Merry couldn't agree with her more.

"For now you'll do well to follow my instructions," said Mistress Webbe.

"I thought I'd made myself clear," said Master Webbe. "The girl is not here for the purpose of maidservant. She is indentured to work at the glasshouse, by order of Captain Norton."

"The glasshouse!" yelled Mistress Webbe. "'Tis all I hear round this place night and day."

Merry shifted uncomfortably from one foot to the other. How she wished they would stop arguing!

"Captain Norton. What does the man know of running a glasshouse? He sends you to England to do all his work, leaving me here in this dreadful swamp. And now he forces us to take in his servant? What makes you think he's been minding the business while you were gone?"

"He's taken ill," said Master Webbe.

"So you say," said Mistress Webbe. "Well, it appears we're stuck with the girl for now. As long as she's here under this roof, she'll be earning her keep, else the almighty Captain Norton can put food in her belly and clothes on her back himself."

"Just take the girl to the loft. She can sleep there," said Master Webbe.

Mistress Webbe shot Merry a sour glance. "Follow me." She and Merry climbed a ladder that led to a loft above the main room.

The space was tiny and dark, and the ceiling so low Merry could not stand up, just as if she were back in the 'tween deck. The walls were rough-hewn logs, with one slit of a window. A straw pallet lay on the floor, and a dusty chest sat in one corner. "They'll come for you directly in the morning to take you to the glasshouse, so you'll need to rise at first light. Make haste and tend to the fire, then set the water to boil in the kettle and collect the eggs." Merry's mind whirled with all she was to remember.

"We can't have you going about in those rags. They look positively indecent." Mistress Webbe rummaged through the chest and gave Merry an old skirt, shift, bodice, and apron to wear. Then she climbed back down the ladder.

The skirt and bodice were of a coarse homespun and scratched Merry around the collar and sleeves. They were a little too big for her, but she hardly took notice. Tomorrow, she would spend the day at the glasshouse! She would gladly work her fingers to the bone if it meant getting to see her friend each day.

For the rest of the day, Merry did as she was told. She raked the henhouse, fed the pigs, and brought carrots, turnips, and pumpkins from the garden for the stew. Merry had never seen pumpkins before. They trailed on vines thick as ship's rope, round and orange as small suns.

She swept the hearth and set the table and fetched wood for the ailing fire. Merry hitched up her skirts before adding a heap of kindling to the coals, then a top log, a fore stick, and a middle stick. But the fire would not catch. At last, with flint and steel, she managed a spark to get it going again.

She could barely stay awake through dinner. Just as she thought she might fall over from exhaustion, Mistress Webbe told her she could go to her bed. But Merry was so tired that she could not sleep. She shivered in the cold night. The scratchy straw that stuffed the pallet poked right through her shift, and she could not escape the smell of the rancid straw.

Blowing out the tallow candle, Merry lay in the dark, listening to strange new sounds. The din of the last croaking frogs, owls softly hooting in the trees, and . . . voices, right below her. Barely louder than a whisper. When Merry raised herself up on her elbow, she could hear Master Webbe talking, but it was not Mistress Webbe who answered in return. It was another man's voice—a voice she had heard many times aboard the *Flying Hart*.

Bernardo! What was he doing at Master Webbe's so

late at night? Merry sat up on her pallet, straining to hear.

"'Twas the first chance I could come. Franz would not stop yammering. He speaks to me as though I know nothing of glassmaking," said Bernardo indignantly.

"Like it or not, he's the master glassblower. You'll have to learn to work with him," said Master Webbe.

"He's not the only problem. The sand here is too gritty for making *cristallo,* just as it was in England. 'Tis not at all like the fine sand we used in Italy. The formula we learned in Venice will not work here," said Bernardo.

Merry heard muffled cursing. Then Master Webbe said, "You'll think of something."

"I'll try. But we'll have to come up with a new formula. Like the one Angelo Lupo was working on when we were in England. Our best hope for a successful formula here is Lupo," said Bernardo.

"Your apprentice?"

Now Merry listened harder.

"Yes. With the others, 'tis just trial and error, and they end up in circles. But Lupo made beads in England that were nearly clear glass. He's hit upon something, but I suspect the materials here may set him back," said Bernardo.

"How can you be certain it wasn't just luck?" asked Master Webbe.

"Lupo has a talent with formulas. He makes notes in his book, *The Art of Glass.* You've seen him on the ship. Those scribbles are part of his formulas," said Bernardo.

"Let's think about this, Bernardo. If your group finds a way to make *cristallo* here in the colony as planned, that's well and good for Captain Norton. He owns the glasshouse, and most of the profits go to him. But what about you and me? That formula would be very, very valuable to us. No one would believe it was discovered by an ordinary apprentice. We could easily claim it for ourselves."

"But Captain Norton would still keep the profits," said Bernardo.

"Leave him to me. He's ill and may soon cease to be a problem," said Webbe. "You get a look at Lupo's book."

"He guards his work well," said Bernardo, "as do all my men. They each want to be named the first to discover the new formula."

"We must find out what he knows. If we can make *cristallo* ourselves and sell it to England, we, Bernardo, shall be very rich men! Have Lupo fetch the girl in the morning. I'd like to have a chat with such a bright lad."

Merry heard the front door open and close. Master Webbe and Bernardo must have stepped outside, where Merry could no longer hear them. She could scarcely believe what they'd been discussing. Master Webbe and Bernardo were plotting to steal Angelo's work.

Merry had to warn him!

CHAPTER 4

THE MISSING BOOK

After a fitful night's sleep, Merry rose before first light. She tended the fire, set the kettle to boil, and gathered the eggs, as Mistress Webbe had instructed. Master Webbe rose just as Angelo came to fetch Merry. She could scarcely contain herself while Master Webbe asked him countless questions. As soon as she and Angelo were alone and well away from the house, Merry poured out what she had heard.

"Angelo! Last night I overheard Bernardo and Master Webbe talking—about the glasshouse, and you! They are plotting to steal the *cristallo* formula from you, and mean to make themselves rich, without benefit to you or Captain Norton. You musn't let that book leave your sight. Guard it well!"

"I've hidden it in my quarters. I won't have a chance to get it until our midday break. There's nothing can be done about it now."

"Master Webbe and Bernardo are no better than snakes hiding underfoot, if you ask me," said Merry.

"If you hope to remain at the glasshouse, you must mind them both. These men, they can cause you harm. Promise me you'll do as they want, Merí."

"Yes, I promise," said Merry.

They continued down the wooded path and soon arrived at Glass House Pointe. Merry and Angelo left the cover of trees and stepped into a clearing. There in the dappled light stood a lone shelter bigger than any house Merry had ever seen, an open-air structure made of sturdy timbers and topped by a thatched roof. The two sides facing the river had walls covered with mud and straw, like barns Merry had seen in England.

Angelo led the way inside. Merry bent her head back and looked up at the sky through the smoke hole piercing the roof. The building was damp and drafty, hardly more than a tent. The floor was nothing more than packed clay. Merry saw tools, barrels, and piles of wood and sand everywhere. She looked for blown glass, but saw only a few small tumblers.

Several other glassmakers arrived and began their work. One put on a leather apron while another took down a long pole from a rack. Then a tall man with a beard called them over. He began measuring some kind of dry ingredients into a clay pot and mixing them together. The other glassblowers watched closely.

When the tall man was finished with his explanation, Angelo took Merry to meet him. "This is Franz Holzer, master glassblower at Jamestown," said Angelo. "And this is Meredith Shipman."

"Merry," she said.

"I welcome you, Merry," said Franz. "You remind me of mine daughter back in Germany." He smiled warmly. "Well, there is certainly work enough here for three of ye."

"I'll do my best," said Merry.

"And I'd best be starting my work," Angelo said, heading for the high table in the far corner.

"We haf only now finished building," said Franz. "There was an old glasshouse on the Pointe many years ago, but it did not succeed. Colonists favored planting and selling the tobacco over glassmaking, I'm afraid, and the whole place fell down. We haf nearly had to start all over.

"At the far table by Angelo, we mix our ingredients. We make glass as I was taught in Germany. *Waldglas*. A dark glass, green as the forest. People can use it every day."

"And what about beads?" asked Merry.

"Beads? The natives favor beads highly for trade. Bernardo and the other Italian men have been brought here to work on making colored beads and other kinds of glass at Jamestown. Blue glass, like the beads you wear, and perhaps even a clear glass."

Cristallo! Merry thought.

"Follow me now, Merry. First you'll need to know how the ovens work," said Franz. At the center of the glasshouse were three round mounds made of river boulders. Off to the side was a fourth, smaller one.

"They look like beehives," said Merry.

"These are the ovens. The fritting furnace you see here is for heating the ingredients at our starting time. The main working furnace over here is for melting the glass. At the far end, our lehr oven is for cooling glass down slowly so that it won't shatter." Pointing to the smaller mound off to the side, he said, "We haf also a kiln where we fire clay pots used to hold our melting glass." He looked at Merry with a furrow in his brow. "You must take care near the ovens, Merry. Often they are very hot and can be danger-ous. Stay back unless I tell you 'tis safe."

"I will," said Merry.

"Fire is a great danger. There are buckets of water all around. The well is right outside. 'Tis your job to see the buckets are filled at all times. There's also a bell—do you see it here?" Merry saw the black iron bell hanging on a post in the corner. "Pull that cord, and men will run here from their quarters, those huts right beyond that row of trees." Merry stood on tiptoe to see the line of roofs Franz was pointing out.

"To make glass, we use potash from wood ashes,

cullet—bits of broken glass—and sand from the beach."

"You make glass from sand?" asked Merry. She could not imagine such a thing.

"Ya." Franz pointed in the direction of the James River. "And I'll need you to haul sand from the beach. I'll also need you to collect wood from the forest or driftwood along the beach. You'll be responsible for sweeping the glasshouse and picking up all broken glass, and you'll need to keep the tools in their proper places as well." Franz pointed out where the pincers and shears, calipers and battledore were kept. Merry concentrated, hoping to keep it all straight.

"I expect steady work from you. Also, stay out from underfoot of the other glassblowers. I am in charge here, so mind that you do as I ask, but remember, all of us answer to Master Webbe. Do you understand?"

Merry nodded.

All morning, Merry swept, hauled wood, and carried buckets of sand. She did not have a chance to speak with Angelo. At noon, while she was eating bread and corn gruel, Angelo sat down beside her. His forehead was creased with concern and his lips pinched tight. He whispered, "Merí, you were right. My book has disappeared. I've looked everywhere. I must try to gain it back from Bernardo, even if I have to search his quarters and steal it back," said Angelo.

"'Twould not be stealing," Merry said firmly. "The book is rightfully yours."

᪰

October soon turned to November, and there was still
no sign of Angelo's book. Angelo searched Bernardo's
sleeping quarters, and those of the other glassmakers, but
with no luck. Merry worried that the book might truly
be lost. She looked for it everywhere—on the way to the
glasshouse each morning, inside the glasshouse as she
swept and returned tools to their proper places, and on
the way to the river to haul sand.

One day on the path to the river, Merry was lost in
thought, turning over the problem of Angelo's missing
book. The air had turned colder, so that she could see her
breath like tiny wisps of fog as she walked.

Merry thought she heard a twig crack behind her. She
stopped walking but heard nothing more. She started
walking, and there it was again. Was someone following
her? Merry peered into the woods, but she could see no
one, no movement but the last red and gold leaves falling
from the trees. Yet she could feel eyes on her. A chill ran
down her spine.

Merry ran the rest of the way through the woods until
she reached the river's edge. She felt safer out in the open
where no one could sneak up on her.

"Who's there? Show yourself," she called into the
woods, but no one appeared.

Was Bernardo keeping watch on her? If Angelo's book

was truly lost, he might think she had it. Were Indians following her? Had she only imagined the sounds?

She walked along the water's edge. Long-necked herons ran from her on stiltlike legs as she bent to shovel sand into her buckets. Merry kept a wary eye on the woods.

As she dug, she found a few perfect clam shells, nesting them like cupped hands inside her pocket. How Margaret would have teased her. Always saving things, collecting smooth river stones, fallen leaves, or bird feathers. Merry picked up a smooth, flat pebble and skipped it across the James River just as she'd done with her sister along the Thames River in London.

Merry shook her head and shoulders, as if to shake off the eyes watching her. When she peered into the forest again she saw a broken branch swaying in the wind, tapping against a tall tree.

How silly to think that someone had followed her, had been spying on her, when all the while it was the wind! She bent to scoop up more sand, turning her mind again to the missing book. Where would Bernardo hide such a thing, if not at the glasshouse or in his own quarters?

That's when the idea came to her. Of course—Master Webbe! *He* could be hiding the book, not Bernardo. Perhaps Bernardo had given it to him for safekeeping, knowing that Angelo would search the glassmakers' huts. Could Angelo's book have been hidden right under her nose these past few weeks?

Now was a perfect time to return to the Webbes' to search for it. Mistress Webbe had taken some cloth to trade with Mistress Norton that morning. Most likely she would stay awhile to gossip. If Merry hurried, Franz would not find her missing for too long. Merry seized the moment and ran back down the path and through the woods, all the way to the Webbes'.

As soon as she arrived at the house, Merry called out "Halloo!" to make certain Mistress Webbe was not home. When no answer came, she hurriedly began her search. First she sorted through Master Webbe's books on the shelf and checked the contents of table drawers. Merry glanced over her shoulder. Had she heard a sound? She stopped to listen, to make certain no one was coming. She rummaged through cupboards, under benches, even inside kettles. Her heart pounded as she lifted the corner of the rug, glancing toward the doorway all the while.

Next she moved to the bed. "God forgive me," she whispered as she slid her hand beneath the Webbes' mattress. Her fingers found something cold and hard. She pulled out a gleaming silver dagger. Merry's heart quickened. What was a dagger doing under Master Webbe's mattress? Merry was not sure she wanted to sleep in the home of a man with a hidden dagger. But she could not stop to dwell on this. She replaced the dagger and continued her search, pawing through chests of linens, bedding, and clothes. The book was nowhere to be found.

But where else was there to look? Merry glanced around the room once more. There was one last chest, but it was covered with Mistress Webbe's special lace cloth, and two heavy candlesticks sat on top. Was there time to search it too? She ran to the window and peered out, then, not seeing anyone, set the candlesticks on the floor, removed the cloth, and lifted the lid.

Merry hurriedly dug through layers of fancy tablecloths, pillow coats, napkins, and towels. Her heart sank. It was no use. She'd spent too much time looking already.

As she was about to give up, Merry's hand struck something hard tucked amid the folds of tablecloths. It felt like a book. She pulled it from among the linens. It was the King James Bible. But why was it hidden? Perhaps it was a special family Bible, stored here for safekeeping. As Merry bent to put it back, she realized it wasn't closed all the way. She opened the Bible to find out why. Inside was Angelo's book! The slim volume had been hidden right inside the Book of Job.

Just then, Merry heard the creak of the outside gate. Her heart hammered. She heard the crunch of leaves, a clearing of the throat. There was no time. The door opened and Mistress Webbe barged in. Merry stood in front of the open chest, holding the Bible. Her cheeks flushed red. She wanted to drop the book and run, but her legs went stiff. Every muscle in her body froze.

"What nonsense is this, creeping about the house in

the middle of the day?" said Mistress Webbe, narrowing her eyes at Merry.

"I was just cleaning up," said Merry. "I found this Bible left out, and I was returning it to the chest where it seems to be kept." She hurriedly replaced the Bible among the folded linens and closed the lid of the chest.

"You have no business here at this hour!"

"I . . . I . . . am here on an errand for Master Webbe," Merry stammered. "He sent me back for his midday slab of meat and slice of bread." Merry was ashamed at how easily the lie came out, but a lie was better than a lashing.

"Master Webbe does not sup at the glasshouse," said Mistress Webbe. "I am about to add vegetables to the roast in the stew pot for his midday meal now."

"I was just following orders," said Merry, trying to sound brave. "I must . . . I need . . ."

"A good lashing is what you need. 'Tis just what shall befall you if Master Webbe finds you here, trying to escape your duties." Mistress Webbe's eyes narrowed once again. "Or have you come to steal? I told Master Webbe this would come to no good. I'll not have a common thief under my roof."

Master Webbe himself is the only thief under this roof! It was all she could do to hold her tongue.

Mistress Webbe pointed to Merry's bulging pocket. "There. What's that you've got hidden in your apron? Do you know what happens to servants caught stealing? Why,

Mistress Taylor had her servant girl tied to a tree for two days for stealing a chicken."

With trembling fingers, Merry reached in her pocket and showed Mistress Webbe her small cache of shells.

Mistress Webbe crossed her arms and made a disapproving sound like a small dog's bark.

"Be off with you to the glasshouse, then. And be glad 'tis not the stocks you're off to. Master Webbe will hear of this, and he'll have your head if you try it again."

Merry left as quickly as she could, hurrying away from the house and the cold glare of Mistress Webbe. She could not wait to tell Angelo what she had discovered.

But the sand buckets! Merry realized she had left them at the river. She had no choice but to go back to the river before heading for the glasshouse. She would be late returning, with little to show for a whole morning's work, and Franz would be angry.

At least she had found the book. Now she had only to steal it back.

CHAPTER 5
HEATING UP

As soon as Merry walked into the glasshouse, Angelo whispered, "Merí, you've been gone all morning. Franz was asking after you. Where have you been?"

With furtive glances over each shoulder, Merry whispered the whole story to Angelo, not forgetting to mention the dagger.

"How can I thank you for finding my book?" he said in a hushed tone. "I thought it was surely gone for good. But sneaking back there, Merí? You shouldn't have! Let's hope the man's dagger is simply for protection against the natives."

Before Angelo could say more, Franz strode up and exclaimed, "Ah, here you are, Merry. Has Angelo told you our news?"

"News?" asked Merry.

"Yes," said Angelo. "Just this morning a gentleman

planter placed our first order for glassware, quite a large order, too. A Mr. Charles Leak, whose land borders that of the glasshouse, behind the glassblowers' huts."

"This is what we haf waited for," continued Franz. "It could make a great difference for us. If Mr. Leak trusts us to blow glass for him right here in Jamestown, then for sure other colonists will also purchase from us, rather than buying glassware from England!"

"The Jamestown glasshouse is going to succeed this time," said Angelo.

"All of the glassblowers must work for long hours. It will be the most glass for us ever to make at one time!" said Franz.

"Goblets and glasses and all manner of bottles," said Angelo excitedly. "Even a linen-smoother and an hourglass, which Franz will have to make specially!"

"Why does a tobacco planter need such a lot of glass?" asked Merry.

"For his new bride," said Angelo.

"Many young women will come to Jamestown on a ship called the *Warwick*," Franz told Merry. "From England they sail. One of them shall be Mr. Leak's bride."

"He wants his household all prepared for her arrival," Angelo said.

" 'Tis a long, hard journey just to find a husband," said Merry, her eyes drifting off as she remembered her own frightening voyage.

"Tobacco brides choose to come," said Angelo. "Of their own free will. Like me, they could be hoping to better themselves."

"This girl shall not be poor, to be sure," remarked Franz, "as long as Englishmen smoke pipes!"

"Or they could be hoping for adventure," Angelo continued. "They are not forced to be . . ."

"Indentured," said Merry angrily, uttering the word Angelo had not wanted to speak. "Just say it." *Better to be a servant than a tobacco bride,* thought Merry. She shuddered at the idea of marrying some man she had never met. What if he proved to be a man like Master Webbe?

"Forgive me, Merí," said Angelo. "I only meant . . . I did not mean to offend you."

"You only spoke the truth," said Merry. Then she added, smiling, "Mr. Leak's bride is sure to have glassware finer than any in England."

"*I'd* hardly call it fine," said Bernardo, interrupting the conversation.

"And what would you call it?" Franz asked.

"Common green, that's what. I cannot imagine why anyone, let alone a wealthy planter, would buy such rude stuff."

"How dare you insult the glass we make in my homeland," said Franz. "I haf been making *Waldglas* since I was an apprentice glassblower in Germany. I suppose you think your fancy glass is better?" He paused, then added

sarcastically, "But one does not know that. I haf not yet
seen the great Bernardo make any glass at all. One wonders
if the great Venetian glassblower really does know how to
blow glass. Or if he simply brags about it."

Bernardo spoke through clenched teeth. "You call me
a liar?"

"We haf yet to see this fine crystal you boast of, these
perfectly clear goblets and beads."

"I cannot help it if the sand here is useless," snarled
Bernardo. "How can we make fine glass if the sand won't
melt down in the right way?"

"It works fine for my purposes," Franz said.

"You dare to challenge me, Holzer? I have blown glass
in the finest centers in Italy and England. You are a simple
craftsman who makes dishes in a crude hut in the woods.
We are as oil and water, you and I."

"Ya, you are correct. Oil and water do not mix."

"Please, no fight," said Angelo, standing between them.
"There is much work to do. You agree, no?"

"Out of the way, Lupo," said Bernardo. "This is not
your business."

"This man insults me in mine own glasshouse," said
Franz. "I haf built ovens from boulders I hauled from the
river with mine own hands. I haf constructed a working
factory where there was only wooded wilderness. I haf
taken raw materials, sand and wood ash, and made them
into something. Trained all these others to blow glass.

More than can be said of the great Bernardo, from what I haf seen."

"If you want a challenge, I'm challenging you," Bernardo told Franz. "I'll use the ingredients you have melting in the ovens, Angelo will assist us, and we'll see who fashions the finer piece of glass."

"Very well," said Franz. He called to one of his glassblowers who was known as the fireman. "Dawson, throw some wood on this fire. Merry, we need some broken glass from out of the corner pit."

Merry hurried to fetch the discarded glass. A competition! She'd caught glimpses of glass being blown as she went about her chores. This would give her a chance to watch glassblowing up close, instead of always having to keep at a distance.

From the far corner table where Angelo was always scraping and grinding, mixing and measuring, he brought over a clay pot that contained more "salts," exact amounts of sand and potash. As Angelo added them to the melting pot, Franz stirred the sticky mess with an iron rake. Then he asked Angelo to add the cullet.

"Why are you adding broken glass?" Merry asked.

"This speeds the melting and blending of ingredients," Franz told her.

The batch was then returned to its place in the oven over a roaring fire, which the fireman kept hot. Some of the other glassblowers stood watching the fire, ready and waiting to assist Franz. When one of them pulled out the melting pot, Merry could see that the sticky mess had turned to white-hot liquid.

"I can't work with all that sand gall," said Bernardo.

Merry turned to Angelo. "What does he mean?"

"See the soapy white scum floating on top?" said Angelo. "'Tis from impurities that rise to the surface." Franz proceeded to skim them off with an iron ladle. Then he dipped out a small amount of the liquid and let it string out into a thread.

Merry's eyes widened. It looked as silken as a strand from a spider's web.

"He's testing the glass," explained Angelo. "To make sure 'tis just the right temperature."

Angelo then dipped a long, hollow iron rod into the melting pot, turned it about, and collected a gather of molten glass at one end. Merry could not take her eyes off the round globe of molten glass that glowed red-hot like a celestial orb, a fiery star.

Rolling the bubble on a polished flat stone to smooth it, Angelo gently blew into the hollow iron, once, twice, and then passed it off to Franz. Franz held the blowing iron to his lips, puffed out his cheeks, and blew the bubble, again and again. After each puff, he removed the rod from his mouth and placed it against his cheek.

"So he does not draw the flame back into his mouth when he breathes," Angelo told Merry.

A hush fell over the room. The other glassblowers stood tense and silent, moving only their eyes. Merry watched with wonder as Franz whirled the rod about his head, lengthening and cooling the glowing bubble. She hardly dared take a breath. Merry even forgot to blink, she was so mesmerized by the dance of the fiery orb.

Then Franz sat on a wooden chair with wide arms. He laid the rod across the arms of the chair and rolled the glass bubble back and forth, stretching the glass, squeezing and twisting it. He handed it to one of the glassblowers to be reheated, then shaped it some more. Merry had never seen anything so wondrous!

Angelo stepped over to the tool rack and picked up another iron rod. "This is the *ponte*," he said as he gathered a small bit of glass from the melting pot and connected the new gather to the bottom of Franz's bottle.

Crack! Franz's beautiful bottle! Merry could not bear to see it broken. Now Bernardo would win for certain.

To her surprise, the bottle wasn't broken at all. Franz had merely cut the glass from the blowing iron with a sharp rap, giving off the popping sound.

Franz used a pair of scissors to trim the lip of the bottle. Angelo stood ready with a forked stick. Balancing the bottle on one end, he carried it to the lehr oven, where it would gradually cool.

If Merry had not seen the process with her own eyes, she would never have believed it. From liquid to fire, then suddenly into glass, green as a new leaf, see-through as a grasshopper's wing.

Following the same steps, Angelo handed off the rod to Bernardo. He lifted up the blowing iron, taking his turn with a gather of glass. He worked faster than Franz, but it looked to Merry as if he merely went through the motions of blowing and shaping the glass. He did not smile or seem to delight in it, as Franz did. He didn't seem to take the care Franz had, as if handling a fragile egg or a bird dropped from its nest. Merry did not see how any bottle made by Bernardo could be as lovely as Franz's. But true to his word, Bernardo's glass was just as splendid—at first sight, that is.

When the glassblowers bent to examine Bernardo's piece, they pointed to the mark made where the bottom of the bottle had broken from the rod. Merry stood on tiptoe, leaning in to see. Angelo pointed out to her that it had the look of a ragged scar rather than a smooth, clean bubble. Merry could see that Bernardo's bottle was a bit tipsy, leaning too far to the left. It reminded her of the men she had seen bowling in the streets when she had first arrived.

Angelo carried Bernardo's bottle to the lehr oven to be cooled.

"Looks as if your contest is no contest at all," mocked Franz. "Unless you wish to challenge me a second time?"

"That's the last you'll see of me blowing the common

green," said Bernardo. "Awful stuff. I'll not be caught again doing your work for you."

"And I won't ask you to, though I do believe this contest was your idea."

"I take my orders from Master Webbe. From me he wants *cristallo,* not your muddy green," said Bernardo.

"I'll not hold my breath for that day to come," said Franz.

" 'Tis closer than you, or anyone, may think," Bernardo said with a scowl.

Thanks to Angelo's stolen book, thought Merry.

"You'll pay for this, Holzer," sneered Bernardo, putting his face so close to Franz's that Merry was sure he could feel Bernardo's hot breath. "There'll come a day, and soon, when you'll be sorry to have doubted me."

Bernardo spat on the ground at Franz's feet and rubbed the dirt with the toe of his boot. Then he turned on his heel and stormed off.

You'll pay for this. Merry heard the echo of Bernardo's words in her mind after he had gone. His voice sounded as cold and hard as gravel, and it made Merry shiver.

"Pay no mind to him," Franz said to Merry. "Can you dig some more clay?" While Angelo carefully arranged the glass pieces in the cooling oven, Franz instructed, "After you're finished, Merry, gather any stones or fragments of pots you might find lying about. We'll need them to cover the working holes in our lehr oven, to control the heat in order for our glass to cool overnight. I'm about to start another batch of glass, so Angelo can show you how when you're ready."

Merry dug and shoveled clay until her hands were muddied and her nails thickened with the deep brown earth. She was happy to have the task. It helped take her mind off Bernardo's warning. When the wooden pail was full, she collected stones just outside the glasshouse, and using her apron as a sling, piled them up in the corner pit.

She looked up to see Angelo balancing a small cruet on the end of the forked stick.

"Aren't you afraid you'll drop it?" asked Merry, keeping her distance.

"Only when someone says so," teased Angelo. He gently set the cruet inside the lehr oven. "Come around behind the oven," he told Merry. "And bring the clay and stones."

Angelo pointed to the oven's working hole, a flared opening at the back, framed in wood. "Press the clay inside the opening, like this, and use it to hold any other rubble you've found. Make sure you fill the holes all the way, to keep some heat inside the oven. The fire's out now, and if the glass cools too quickly, it will shatter."

Merry did just as she was told, until not a crack of light peeked through the clay. When Franz and his men finished blowing glass for the day, Franz plugged up the working holes in the other ovens so they would stay hot until tomorrow.

Before she left, Merry picked up glass threads and bits

of broken glass from the day. She tossed the cullet into the corner pit. But a few pieces were too beautiful to throw away. Tying thread around the splinters of glass, she hung them from a low beam where they caught the light and the wind. They made a pleasant sound, soothing as a waterfall, musical as the tinkling of a small bell. Then Merry watered and swept the dirt floor before the waning autumn light made it impossible to see.

It had been a long day, full of argument, yet she could hardly wait till morning, when the first of Franz's glass for Mr. Leak would be finished. She thought of the magic she had seen. Making glass was like turning fire to ice. Merry longed to touch it, to hold a tumbler, a glass, and raise it to the light as if she held a star in the palm of her own small hand.

Chapter 6

The Midnight Visitor

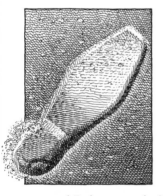

M erry arrived back at the Webbes' that evening, weary but happy from the day. Franz may have overlooked Merry's absence that morning, but Mistress Webbe had not forgotten.

As soon as Merry stepped through the door, Mistress Webbe informed her husband, "That girl is a no-good sneak, and I daresay she's a thief. Just this morning I caught her pawing through our chests. She came here in the middle of the day, trying to steal, I tell you. Then she plainly told a bold-faced lie about it! Right to my face, mind you."

"I'd rather not discuss this without my supper," Master Webbe growled. His eyes looked red and bleary, and Merry knew this meant he'd had one too many of his fermented pumpkin ales.

"'Tis not nearly ready," snapped Mistress Webbe.

Master Webbe snarled, "I'll not be coming home to an empty house and an empty table!"

"Your supper's not ready for one reason. The girl is long overdue from the glasshouse and should have had the hasty pudding set to boiling long ago. She's much to account for this day, if you ask me."

Merry put on her apron and scurried to scald and scour the kettle Mistress Webbe had used for cheese making. She was ordered to complete her chores, then sent to her bed without supper.

"And ye should be glad of it," complained Mistress Webbe. "What other master would not have you flogged?"

Merry did not have a single chance to get Angelo's book. It was just as well. She was so tired she hardly felt the strength to lift the lid of the chest. She collapsed onto her bed and slept the night through without having removed so much as her shoes.

෴

Merry was startled awake by the din of the first thrush calling to its mate. She sensed it was nearly morning, and climbed down the ladder with less noise than a church mouse. *Creak!* She stopped cold. But the house was dark as a barn in winter, and the only sound now was the breathing of the Webbes as they slept.

She crept across the floor, praying that the Webbes would not awaken. Even the swoosh of her skirt sounded too loud. Instead of starting the fire, she tiptoed over to the blanket chest, silently removed the candlesticks and lace, and lifted the Bible from under the quilts.

Something was different. The Bible was in its proper place, but Merry could feel that it was closed tight. Angelo's book was gone!

Merry searched the chest, groping through the folds of blankets. The book was no longer in the chest. The Webbes would awaken at any moment. What else could she do? She closed the chest, then started the fire, swept the hearth, collected the eggs, and set the kettle to boil. As she went about her chores, she wondered where the book had gone. Mistress Webbe had told her husband that Merry had looked through the blanket chests. He must have known the hiding place was no longer safe. *Maybe he hid the book under his mattress, with the dagger,* Merry thought with a shudder.

Merry hurried from the house before the Webbes arose.

Feathers of red clouds streaked the early-November sky. The now-familiar call of the red-winged blackbird echoed through the woods. With each step toward the glasshouse, her heart lifted and the heaviness in her shoulders and feet felt lighter.

Merry remembered that first day when she'd thought the glasshouse was nothing more than a rude hut in the forest. In hardly more than a month's time, it had become more home to her than any place had been in months. How could she not love a place where sand was made liquid,

liquid turned to fire, and fire to glass, as if by magic. She could hardly wait for Franz and Angelo to arrive and reveal the newly blown glass from the cooling oven.

She did not even mind the hard work, for here was a place where she was trusted to do a good job, where she was not considered a thief and a liar.

By the time Merry reached the glasshouse, she was chilled to the bone. Another crisp fall morning, and she'd left the Webbes' in such a hurry she'd forgotten her cloak. If only she had a bit of porridge to warm her from the inside. No matter. The glasshouse ovens would soon warm her. But this morning, the glasshouse felt as cold as the outside air.

Work would get her blood moving, Merry decided. She knelt in front of the main working furnace to pick up a glass dripping. Franz had cautioned her countless times not to get too close to the ovens. But Merry felt no warmth at all. No heat radiated from the oven. She walked right up to the oven and set her hand against one of its round boulders.

Stone cold.

She walked over to the fritting furnace, the one that heated ingredients. It too was cold. Yet Merry knew that Franz had fired both ovens last night so they would hold their temperature today. If the ovens were cold, no glass could be blown for days! And what about the lehr oven, where all Franz's beautiful glass was cooling? Just yesterday she'd plugged up the working hole with clay and rubble so the oven would cool slowly. She ran to the lehr oven and felt it. Not the least bit warm. Was that the way it was supposed to be? She walked around to the back to check the working hole. Rubble and clay were scattered on the ground, leaving a yawning, gaping hole!

Could Franz have arrived ahead of her and removed the clay himself? Merry held the back of her hand to the opening and felt a draft of air so chill that the hairs on her arm stood on end. If Franz had just recently opened the working hole, wouldn't it still be warm?

Merry leaned over and peered as best she could into the dark hole. She thought she saw shapes, outlines that could be the necks of bottles, the stems of glasses. Perhaps the glassware would be all right.

Merry carefully stretched an arm through the working hole and pulled out a glass. It crumbled to pieces in her hand. She lifted out a bottle by its neck, and it too shattered in her hand. Goblets and bottles that shattered at the touch!

Merry ran to the back of each oven, checking the working holes. In each case, the hole was wide open. She could see the clay and rubble strewn on the ground. Someone had removed all the clay and stone from each hole during the night and let the ovens go cold.

Was Bernardo getting back at Franz for the contest? Merry searched the ground in back of the ovens, hoping to find anything the intruder might have left behind. She had swept the dirt floor clean the night before, but now she noticed a clear footprint cast in the clay floor directly behind the lehr oven. It was large and squared off at the toe but had a distinct shape at the bottom, as if part of the heel had broken off.

She had to find Franz. She hurried down the rutted path toward the glassmakers' quarters. Franz met her on his way up, with Angelo close behind.

"Franz!" she shouted. "Angelo! Hurry! Something's happened at the glasshouse. Something is terribly wrong." As the three ran back up the path to the glasshouse, Merry explained what she had found. She led them over to the lehr oven first and showed them the working hole.

Franz touched each of the ovens. "Cold. Cold as a frosted pumpkin."

Angelo touched the ovens himself. "These have been cold for some time," said Angelo. "Perhaps all night."

"How can this be? I know I built up heat in the fire chamber before I left last night," said Franz. "Someone must haf come back in the night."

"But why bother the ovens?" asked Angelo.

"I haf my own idea about that," said Franz, his jaw tightening. "We cannot make glass today. 'Twill be days before our ovens again reach temperature. Angelo, go and empty the cooling oven. See if anything can be salvaged."

Angelo opened the oven door to a sorry sight. A carpet

of glass, green and broken, littered the floor of the oven like fallen leaves.

Franz's face fell.

There were a few pieces left standing. Franz reached in and gently pulled out a glass. It shattered at his touch.

"Brittle as a dry stick," said Franz. "Someone meddled with the holes soon after I left. The glass had no time to strengthen. Some of it exploded right inside the oven."

"Oh, Franz, all your beautiful glass—shattered!" Merry said.

"I must get him for this," Franz muttered. "Merry, help Angelo with sweeping up the glass. I haf something to do. I shall not be gone too long."

Angelo rekindled a fire in the main oven while Merry swept up the glass. She broke the silence.

"Your book is no longer in Master Webbe's chest. Mistress Webbe told him she'd caught me looking there, so he probably moved it to a new hiding place."

"Leave it be, Merí. Much of that formula comes from up here," said Angelo, tapping his head. "They can't steal that from me."

"I'm glad," said Merry. "What will happen now when Franz finds Bernardo?"

"If I know Bernardo, he is sure to accuse someone else!" said Angelo. "He never takes the blame."

"Only the credit. Without doing any of the hard work himself," said Merry. "'Tis not fair. You're the one making beads that are nearly clear glass!"

"They won't stop me just by taking my book, I promise you. I even mean to experiment with cobalt and fashion some blue beads for that necklace of yours. How I hope I can make some the color of the Venetian sky someday."

"Here, then," said Merry, slipping another of the beads from her necklace and handing it to Angelo. "Keep this for inspiration."

Angelo tucked the bead into his pocket. "I promise you I will protect this."

"Take care of yourself, too, Angelo," said Merry. "Bernardo may be dangerous."

Merry and Angelo looked at each other gravely. Merry knew they were both recalling Bernardo's angry words: *You'll pay for this.*

CHAPTER 7

HOT AND COLD

After Merry swept up all the shattered glass, she took her basket and walked down the path toward the river to collect driftwood. She'd only gone a few steps when she heard voices. Loud, shouting voices.

"You cannot keep me from blowing glass just because you're a sloth and won't do any work yourself," Franz said angrily. "I'll not haf you sneaking around behind mine back, fooling with mine ovens again."

"*Your* ovens!" shouted Bernardo. "You sound as if you own the place. We'll see what Captain Norton has to say about that."

Merry rounded the corner to find Franz and Bernardo on the brink of a fistfight.

"You will find yourself on the next boat back to England or Italy or wherever it was you came from," said Franz. "Just as soon as he finds out you haf destroyed all his glassware and kept me from my work."

"I didn't destroy anything, you miserable gaffer," said Bernardo, throwing a punch at Franz. Franz held his jaw. Merry was afraid he'd had a tooth knocked out by the blow. Franz rushed at Bernardo, knocking him to the ground.

"Angelo! Come quick!" called Merry, running back toward the glasshouse. "Franz and Bernardo. They're fighting! Someone is sure to get hurt. We've got to do something."

Angelo ran over to them and tugged at Franz while two of the other glassblowers stepped in to help separate the men. "Fools!" shouted Angelo. "You could both hang."

"Quick!" cried Merry. "'Tis Master Webbe, with Captain Norton! I've seen them just now through the trees, heading this way!"

Franz rubbed his jaw while Angelo helped Bernardo to his feet. They entered the glasshouse through the back, just as Master Webbe and Captain Norton came out of the woods.

When they entered the glasshouse, Franz greeted them as if he had not just been in the middle of a brawl. "Captain Norton! To what do we owe this pleasure?"

"Captain Norton has just been informed of the order of glassware from Mr. Leak. We've come to check on its progress," said Master Webbe.

"Yes," said Captain Norton, coughing deep in his

chest. "I've heard good things about your glassblowing, Holzer, and now that construction of the glasshouse is finished, I've come to see your wares for myself."

"I'm very pleased, sir," said Franz. "We haf been waiting for your arrival."

"I would have checked on your progress sooner, what with the arrival of the new men, but for my ill health." He coughed again, as if it was an effort to speak. "Please, excuse me."

Merry ran outside to fetch him a mug of water from the well. *What will Franz tell them?* she wondered.

Merry offered Captain Norton the water, then tried to go about her chores as usual. She heard Franz say, "I'm sorry, Captain Norton. I haf nothing to show you as yet."

Before he could explain any further, Captain Norton exclaimed, "What's this? Do you mean to say you've not begun the glass for Mr. Leak?" He turned to Master Webbe. "Webbe, what is the meaning of this? I told you I'd hold you accountable, and I mean to."

Master Webbe then turned on Franz. "To my knowledge, the order was well under way a few days ago. I demand to know why 'tis not now even begun."

"Yesterday, many types of glass were finished for planter Leak," said Franz. "But this morn, Merry has arrived and found our ovens tampered with." Franz threw a scowl at Bernardo.

"What can you mean?" asked Captain Norton.

"Last night, after I had left the glasshouse, it would appear someone sneaked back and took out all the clay from our working holes," said Franz. "Our glass cooled too quickly, became brittle, and crumbled into pieces."

"Someone must know something of this," said Master Webbe. "Ovens do not cool and glass crumble to bits all by themselves!"

"Why do we not ask *him*," said Franz, nodding in Bernardo's direction.

"I know nothing of this," claimed Bernardo. "I have nothing to do with this order of planter Leak's. 'Tis not I who makes the common green. For all I know, could be the natives wreaking havoc in the night!"

Merry fumed inside herself.

"Can the servant girl have gotten it wrong?" asked Captain Norton.

His words stung her. Merry's ears reddened and her face flushed, as if she were standing too close to a fire. "If you please, Captain Norton," said Merry, "I did just as I was told."

Angelo stepped in, speaking up on Merry's behalf. "Angelo Lupo, sir. I showed her how to plug the holes myself, then checked to see that she'd done it properly."

"Perhaps you overlooked something," said Master Webbe, scowling at Angelo. "Perhaps you thought—"

"I know my work, sir," interrupted Angelo. "And I do it well."

"And you'll do well not to speak when you are being spoken to," warned Master Webbe, quick to knock Angelo down a rung. His purplish scar stood out from his cheek like a twisted old grapevine.

"Yes, sir," said Angelo.

Merry wished the dreadful man would take his wife and go back to England, even if it meant that Merry had no place to live. She wanted to scream! Instead, she appealed to Captain Norton. "Please understand," she said, "I am grateful to work at the glasshouse. I would never do anything to work against it, nor would Angelo."

"We'll hear no more excuses today!" said Master Webbe. "If I catch anyone tampering with these ovens, they'll pay with their life."

Captain Norton coughed until he was red in the face. Merry saw blood on the handkerchief he held over his mouth. When the spell was over, he said, "Webbe, I've put you in charge of this venture. You've got new men to train and glass to make, so I want to know there'll be no repeat of this. Post guard if necessary. If the culprit is caught, see that he pays dearly."

"Holzer, you'll stay awake and guard the glasshouse at night," Master Webbe ordered Franz.

"I'm holding you responsible, Webbe," repeated Captain Norton. "We've a glasshouse to run, and I expect no more of this nonsense."

Merry saw Master Webbe's eyes flash, but he said

nothing in return. At the entrance to the glasshouse, he stopped and turned as if to have one last word, but no words came. Finally, he continued down the piney path with nothing more than a flick of his cape.

After the two men left, Merry found her broom and swept furiously. As she swept the main entrance, she noticed a fresh print in the mud right near the glasshouse entryway—a clear print pointing down the trail, with a crescent moon where a chunk of the heel had broken off.

The print had to belong to Captain Norton or Master Webbe. They were the only two who had recently left the glasshouse by that door. *Captain Norton has no reason to sabotage his own glassworks,* Merry thought. *But what of Master Webbe?*

Some of the other glassblowers were working to get the fires going again in the ovens. Merry asked one of them if he knew where Angelo was. "I saw him out back," said one, "washing cullet at the well." Merry found Angelo and quickly told him about the footprint she'd just seen and how it matched the one behind the ovens.

"It could be Master Webbe's," said Angelo. "But it could also belong to Bernardo or anyone, no? We all come and go countless times a day. What did it look like?"

Picking up a stick, Merry traced an outline of the boot in the dirt, with the squared-off toe and the broken heel.

"Bernardo's boots are like mine," said Angelo. "Not squared at the top."

Merry felt sure the print was Master Webbe's. She planned to have a look at his boots the first chance she got.

That evening on her way home, Merry thought of poor Franz, who would be spending the night shivering in the glasshouse loft, awaiting the intruder. *There won't come any mischief now,* she thought. For it looked as if the man who had ruined the green glass was the same man who'd given the order for the glasshouse to be watched. *Clever,* thought Merry.

Still, she had to be sure. And the boot print could prove it. But as soon as Merry arrived back at the house, Mistress Webbe kept her busy with the cooking and the fire. Merry found herself climbing the ladder to bed, and Master Webbe had yet to take off his boots. Next morning, she'd try to awaken before the Webbes and hope that Master Webbe had left his boots by the door.

CHAPTER 8

UNDER THE SAME ROOF

 erry awoke earlier than usual
the next morning. But when
she climbed down softly from the loft,
she saw that a fire already burned in
the hearth, and a sour smell instantly
reached her nose—the medicinals that
Mistress Webbe often brewed. Why
was she already awake?

Merry spied the boots by the door. She saw her chance.
Her heart thumped wildly. She picked up one of the boots
and, after glancing over her shoulder, turned the boot
over. Nothing. She quickly inspected the other. The heel
was caked with dried mud. Merry brushed off the mud
with her apron. A chunk of mud fell away, and she could
see where part of the heel was broken off, in a perfect
crescent moon.

"There you are. At last," said Mistress Webbe. Merry
jumped, dropping the boot.

"What are you doing, girl?" asked Mistress Webbe,

picking up the boot and waving it in front of Merry. "What business have you with Master Webbe's boots? I told you not to bother his things."

"I thought I'd give these a cleaning," Merry lied.

"Never mind that," said Mistress Webbe. "Look at your apron. 'Tis a sorry sight. And you've gone and got mud all over the floor. Clean up this mess and be off with you to the glasshouse."

Minutes later, Merry gladly hurried down the path to the glasshouse. The walk gave her a chance to quiet her thumping heart. She hardly minded Mistress Webbe's scolding—at least she'd discovered the owner of the broken-heeled boot. She wished she had some *real* proof—the bootprints were surely gone by now, trampled by the feet of glassblowers arriving for work this morning.

Franz posted watch, and just as Merry suspected, the troublemaker stayed away. Merry welcomed the peace. Three weeks had passed and the ovens had reached temperature once more. Nothing made Merry happier than to see glass being blown again. She could not help stopping her work to admire a spout being made on a beaker or decorations that looked like raspberries being formed on the stem of a drinking glass.

Best of all, Franz made special bottles to hold oils,

spirits, powders, perfumes, and medicines for Mr. Leak and his bride-to-be. Each had its own seal on the front, raised and round as a silver shilling and bearing the letters *CML,* which were Mr. Leak's initials. Merry lifted a bottle and traced the smooth, raised *M* with her finger, knowing it well from the start of her own name.

Another cold snap hit Jamestown, yet the glasshouse ovens warmed her, as did the work. There was a comforting rhythm to her daily chores—raking ashes, tending fires, digging clay, washing sand. Then one rare, sun-slanted afternoon in late November, Franz made Merry an unexpected offer.

"I haf seen how you admire the bottles with special seals," said Franz. "If you could work doubly hard and finish your duties early, you could help extra by learning how to mix sand and potash in the crucible."

"Do you mean it? I know I can learn," said Merry.

"Good. Tomorrow, you shall stay late, and Angelo will teach you to measure. For your work, I promise to make a special bottle that you may keep for yourself. It will bear a seal with your very own initials. What is your middle name, Merry?"

"I wish I knew," said Merry. "My parents died, and I was too young to have a memory of my middle name."

"Well, the letters *MS* it must then be, for Meredith Shipman."

"Thank you!" said Merry. Tired as she was at the day's

end, she could not wait to begin the extra work Franz
needed done. Besides owning a glass bottle of her very
own, she'd be happy to be away from the Webbes' for an
extra hour each day.

But the next morning, as soon as she had dressed and
climbed down from the loft, Mistress Webbe greeted her
with bad news.

"You're not to go to the glasshouse this morning."

"But I must—"

"There'll be no argument. 'Tis Master Webbe's bidding."

"I just wanted . . . I had hoped . . ."

" 'Tis time you learned to be done with wanting and
hoping. I had hoped to be back in England by now, but
you've yet to see me sail."

Mistress Webbe's endless talk of England made Merry
more weary than her chores did. Merry had grown quite
fond of Jamestown. She had work she loved and people
she cared about. True, the Webbes were heartless and cold,
but at least Mistress Webbe's warm corn cakes and the
occasional bits of bacon or ham were better than racing
pigeons for crumbs of bread in the backstreets of London.

Was Master Webbe punishing Merry? Did he know
she suspected him? Merry could hardly imagine a worse
punishment than being stuck in this dreary house all day
under Mistress Webbe's watchful eye. Her and her foul-
smelling brews!

Mistress Webbe rapped Merry's hand with a wooden

spoon to get her attention. "You'll do well to listen when you're being spoken to!" said Mistress Webbe.

Merry rubbed her stinging hand. "I'm sorry. I was—"

"Somewhere else, I daresay. As soon as this is done brewing, you leave for Captain Norton's."

"Captain Norton's?"

"Haven't you heard a word I've said, girl? Mistress Norton has been called upon to pay respects to some of her relatives at Martin's Hundred, down the James River. She will not be taking young Thomas on the journey."

Merry could not see what this had to do with her, and why she would not be going to the glasshouse that day.

"Captain Norton is still quite ill, so he will not make the journey. You will be freed from your duties at the glasshouse to look after young Thomas and take care of the captain for a short while. You'll be staying the nights there until Mistress Norton returns home."

It was all Merry could do to keep her mouth shut. Why did they have to send her away from the glasshouse?

"I've some medicinals for you to take to Captain Norton as well. Dr. Pott will be looking in on him each day. Mind you, keep those light fingers of yours to yourself. I'll not have them wagging tongues about you pinching bread from Captain Norton."

One thing she would not miss—the sharp tongue of Mistress Webbe.

Merry could no longer hold her own tongue. "But what

of Mistress Norton's own maidservant? Surely she can look after the boy better than I."

"'Tis not yours to question. But if you must know, she is needed to accompany Mistress Norton on her journey."

Merry knew there was no use protesting. She packed up her things and left for Captain Norton's.

∽

When she arrived, Thomas showed her where she would sleep. Her bed was in a back alcove, all to itself. Cheerful curtains hung in a window of her very own. Next to the bed was a small table, on which Mistress Norton had left a bottle with some dried leaves and flowers, and a soap cake that smelled of bayberry.

Dr. Pott came by later in the morning.

"I'll take Thomas outside," Merry told him. "Fresh air will do us both good."

"Mind you're back soon," said the doctor. "Captain Norton must not be left alone."

Despite the early-December day, the sun warmed Merry's back as they strolled along. She scooped up acorns and showed Thomas their funny hats. Thomas found a forked stick and searched for copper-bellied snakes, even though Merry assured him they would be hiding for the winter. She and Thomas had come nearly all the way to Glass House Pointe when Thomas pleaded, "Play hide-

and-seek with me, Merry."

Merry hid behind a rock, and Thomas found her right away. But when Thomas hid, Merry could not find him among the trees.

She stood still and listened. Where was that boy?

Then Merry heard Master Webbe's voice coming down the path. He was talking with Bernardo. She hid behind a stand of pines so they wouldn't catch sight of her.

"'Tis not going to be as easy as I thought," said Bernardo.

"You have Lupo's book," said Master Webbe. "Why can't you get the formula to work? You said he was close."

Thieves! If only I'd been a moment quicker the day I found that book in the chest, Merry thought.

"I need more information from him. I checked the notes he's keeping now, but he's not much further than he was in the book," said Bernardo. "He's working from memory now. Perhaps if he had the book back, he could make progress more quickly . . . I could have it turn up, as if it had been misplaced."

"He'll suspect something," growled Master Webbe.

"He may already suspect," said Bernardo, "the way he whispers with the girl."

"Never mind her," said Master Webbe. "'Tis Lupo we have to think about."

Merry stood rigid. She dared not take a breath.

"He's nearly there," said Bernardo. "I'm certain of it."

"See that you get what we're after, and quickly," said Master Webbe. "Then he won't be needed any longer and we'll get him out of the way."

Out of the way! thought Merry. Would they go so far as to hurt Angelo? She thought of Master Webbe's dagger. She had to warn Angelo somehow.

Master Webbe was the one speaking now. *"Cristallo* will be the thing that sets us apart from all the world, save Italy. We'll never make much money with the common green. 'Tis hardly worth shipping to England."

Merry tiptoed from her hiding spot and crept away to find Thomas. She had to take him home so she could tend Captain Norton. Dr. Pott would be gone by now. There'd be no chance to get word to Angelo today.

❧

"Let's play Game of the Goose. Or marbles," said Thomas as soon as they arrived back at the Nortons'.

"Thomas," Merry snapped. "Can't you sit still for one moment?" She had to think of a way to warn Angelo.

When Merry saw Thomas hanging his head, she said, "I'm sorry, Thomas. Go ahead and take out your game. Dr. Pott has gone for today. 'Tis time for your father's herbals. Let me take him his brew, and then we'll play."

Merry boiled ale in the kettle and added the herbs that Mistress Webbe had sent with her, along with flowers and berries, turning the drink into a vile-smelling remedy.

She had to tell Angelo that he must stop work on the *cristallo*. Bernardo had been spying on his work, and if Angelo got any closer, Bernardo would finish the formula himself and get Angelo "out of the way."

She took the brew in to Captain Norton, who appeared to be sleeping, or at least dozing between fits of shivering. From the sweat on his brow, Merry could tell that he had a high fever, and a raspberry-red rash spotted his face. He struggled to say something to Merry that sounded like, "Drink . . . no . . . more."

It was no wonder that he refused the brew. The smell was enough to turn any stomach. Merry left the room and went to find Thomas. He had taken out his game board but sat staring at the seeds they used for markers.

"I wish my father would play the game with me."

"I know, Thomas. But your father is very sick. We all hope he'll be well soon."

Between the attention she had to give to Thomas and nursing Captain Norton, the day flew by. At last, Merry put Thomas to bed and had a moment's peace.

How could she sneak to the glasshouse to warn Angelo? The only chance she'd have to get away from the Nortons' would be during Dr. Pott's visit the following morning. Merry would have to take Thomas with her. She'd tell the doctor that she had been instructed by Captain Norton to get a report on the progress of Mr. Leak's order. She'd say extra prayers for the lie and hope that God would forgive her.

⚜

The next morning, Merry called out Thomas's name as soon as she awakened and set the fire. No answer. Perhaps Thomas was hiding again.

"Thomas!" Merry called again as she tried to smother a spark that caught the hem of her skirt. Thomas did not come running. Where had the little devil gotten to? She had to find him before Dr. Pott arrived.

Merry looked in all his usual places. No Thomas. She ran out to look in the garden. There was no sign of Thomas anywhere. Suddenly, Merry felt frantic. She raced inside to tell his father. "Captain Norton!" she said, but he did not wake. "Captain Norton!" she nearly shouted.

Captain Norton lay still on his bed. The flush of fever and the rose of his rash had disappeared. He looked ghost-like, so motionless that it sent a chill through Merry.

"Captain Norton," she pressed, nearly crying now. She shook his shoulder, but he felt cold to the touch and still did not open his eyes.

Merry leaned over him, then jumped back with a gasp. Blood soaked the pillow and the bed linen. Perhaps he had coughed up blood in his sleep. His mouth was still open. Merry held the back of her hand to his mouth. No breath.

Captain Norton was dead!

Merry sprinted for the Webbes', her heart pounding. No one was at home! She ran the rest of the way into town, not thinking about the cold air that stabbed at her. She twisted her ankle on the rutted road but kept running, past the storehouse, through the public square, until she reached Dr. Pott's house. She pounded on the door until he woke up and came with her.

As they hurried back to the Nortons', Merry caught a glimpse of Thomas's sandy-colored head behind a tree alongside the path. She had not known Captain Norton long, but she felt the sadness and weight of his death in the slump of Thomas's shoulders, in the tearfulness of his eyes. She ran to Thomas and held him close.

"Thomas! You had me frantic with worry."

"My father! He won't wake up! I ran and hid when I saw him like that."

Merry could hardly find words. "Thomas, I'm so sorry. Your father was very sick. You're right, Thomas—he isn't going to wake up. I'm afraid he died in his sleep."

"*No!*" shouted Thomas. His eyes darted this way and that, as if he were looking for another place to run off to. Merry took his hand and led him back to the house. Thomas squeezed her hand as if he'd never let go. He cried and cried. She tried her best to comfort him.

Each hour felt like a day to Merry until Mistress Norton returned home. She cradled her son in her arms and mopped his tears with the hem of her apron.

"I'm so sorry" was all Merry could think to say.

"Thank you, my dear," said Mistress Norton. "I know not how to thank you for all you've done for my Thomas." She squeezed Merry's hand in her own.

Merry was asked over and over to tell just how she'd come to find Captain Norton that morning. When Merry told the story, she no sooner mentioned the blood upon the pillow than people's eyebrows raised. In no time, tongues began to wag. Some people said the illness had not taken him at all. All that blood, they said. Surely it meant Captain Norton had been stabbed in the night!

As Merry tossed and turned in her own bed that night, she tried to take her mind off the image of the dagger under Master Webbe's bed. She did not like Master Webbe nor trust him, but would he really kill a man?

Master Webbe had everything to gain, Merry realized. With Captain Norton gone, Master Webbe would probably try to take over the glasshouse. Then he and Bernardo could do as they pleased. They would get Angelo out of the way as soon as Bernardo had what was needed from him. There would be no stopping them.

To think of it, thought Merry as she tossed fitfully, *a would-be murderer right under my own roof!*

CHAPTER 9

ANGELO ACCUSED

Merry welcomed her return to the glasshouse the next morning. At last, she'd be able to warn Angelo of the danger he was in. She met him on the path outside the glasshouse.

"I've only just heard about the death of Captain Norton," Angelo said. "Merí, how are you now?"

"I'm fine," said Merry, though she trembled just thinking about finding Captain Norton dead.

"I've something to show you," said Angelo. He pulled a bead from his pocket that was crystal clear. *"Cristallo!* My formula is working at last. I hope 'twas not just a happy accident. 'Tis only one bead, but 'tis the first clear glass in the New World."

"Angelo, no!" whispered Merry urgently. "You musn't show that to anyone! 'Twill put you in great danger. Master Webbe and Bernardo, I overheard them. They want you out of the way as soon as you discover *cristallo!*"

Angelo stood stock-still. He did not say a word. Merry heard the familiar crunch of leaves underfoot. She caught a glimpse of Bernardo's bulky form moving out from behind the stack of wood and heading down the path. Had he been spying on them? Was he headed off to tell Master Webbe?

As soon as she could be certain he'd gone, she continued, "We must be careful! Some are saying Captain Norton did not die of an illness at all. Maybe Master Webbe used his dagger to stab Captain Norton, and he'll use it to kill you, too, now that you have the formula!"

Just then, Franz came up the path. "No speaking of this any longer," said Angelo.

"Promise me you'll be on guard," Merry pleaded. "Keep the *cristallo* to yourself for now. And watch your back at all times!"

"Merry!" said Franz. "I welcome you back."

Merry turned around. "Thank you. I've been missing this place," she said.

"I am sorry to hear about Captain Norton," said Franz. "He was a good man."

"'Tis a sad time for Mistress Norton and young Thomas," said Merry with a sigh.

"Come inside, Merry. I haf something to cheer you up," said Franz.

Merry stepped inside and looked around her. Rows and rows of beautiful glass! Light poured through the green glass the way it filtered through a church window. Goblets and tumblers, perfume and sweet-water bottles, swirled bottles and fluted glasses with fine stems gleamed on the shelves.

Merry picked up a round tumbler, circling the smooth rim with her finger. 'Twas as if Franz had taken a stream in spring and stopped it in time, so that Merry could hold it in her hand.

Franz's eyes danced as he showed Merry the glass for Mr. Leak's order. Seeing all the glass pieces together took her breath away.

"No more incidents?" Merry asked anxiously.

"None," said Franz. "I must haf scared our intruder away, with all those nights I haf been keeping watch."

"You've certainly been busy in my absence!" said Merry.

Angelo joined them. "Let me show you what else I've been working on," he said as he reached into his pouch and held out a handful of blue glass beads.

"Angelo!" cried Merry. "They're just like my necklace."

"I am sorry, Merí, but I can't find the bead you gave me," replied Angelo.

"No matter," Merry replied. "These are just as lovely."

"Not quite. The mineral I used, cobalt, made a close match, but yours are real Venetian beads. They have a deeper, more even color. Just think, Merí. Soon we'll be able to make blue bottles and glasses and such."

Merry held up a bead, and it twinkled in the light.

"'Tis as if you've plucked the stars from the heavens! How can I ever thank you?"

"If you wear them round your neck," said Angelo. "Here, let me string them on your necklace." Merry untied the cord, and Angelo worked at stringing the new beads.

"*Perfetto,*" said Angelo after he had knotted the cord once more around Merry's neck. He grinned with pride. "Now, we'd best resume our work. Master Webbe has made it quite clear our glassmaking must go on without delay, despite Captain Norton's death."

"I am not surprised," said Merry. "He does not want all eyes turned upon him. But this is one pair of eyes that shall be watching him like a hawk."

Several nights later, Merry distinctly heard a door open, then close. Despite her bare feet, she tiptoed downstairs to peer from a window. There he was! Master Webbe himself, wearing his dark cloak, sneaking silently away from the house and off into the black night.

Merry threw on her own cloak and laced her shoes as quickly as she could. She ran until she saw the outline of the cloak in the moonlight, like a shadow stealing away, aiming straight for the forest.

Did she dare follow? She could not help remembering

the silver dagger. Yet her feet kept moving, running, following, and her heart kept pounding. Her breath formed tiny clouds in front of her as she ran.

She followed him down the path, hoping the crunch of pine needles underfoot would not give her away. When Master Webbe stopped in the path to listen, Merry darted behind a tree. The moment she thought she heard footsteps again, she stepped out from behind the tree.

Where had he gone? She ran along the path. He'd been going in the direction of the glasshouse, but Merry could not catch sight of the cloak.

Did he know she had followed? Was he hiding in the shadows, waiting to grab her?

Merry stopped in her tracks. She couldn't bear to think what would happen if Master Webbe found her following him in the dark of midnight.

She turned and fled back up the path the way she had come, not stopping to look behind her until she reached the Webbes' door.

Merry never heard Master Webbe return that night. Desperate to stay awake, she tried counting her beads, but she was so tired it was no use. She fell into a deep sleep.

At first light, she hurried to start her chores. She was worried about what she might find at the glasshouse. The Webbes were already awake. Master Webbe was seated at the table near the hearth. Mistress Webbe held her husband's cloak in her hand.

"Look here!" she cried. "Your cloak caught on something and ripped right through. How could you be so careless? I work my fingers to the bone with all that needs mending round here!"

"Give it over to me, woman. I need to wear it today. I'll have no more of your god-awful screeching," said Master Webbe.

Merry took advantage of their argument and slipped out the door unnoticed. She ran full speed through the woods until she reached the glasshouse. When she stepped inside, she saw that the shelves stood empty. Broken glass was scattered all across the floor. Every last beaker and bottle—smashed to bits. Merry could have wept. All Mr. Leak's glass, everything Franz had worked so hard for, was gone. Had Master Webbe done this?

Merry studied the shelves. They were set off in the corner, where the finished glassware would be kept out of the way. Surely no one could have bumped the shelves by mistake. And they were shielded from the wind, so the glass could not have been blown over.

Merry sounded the bell at once. Franz and all the other glassblowers came running. They stood around in bitter silence, staring at the sea of broken glass.

"Where's Bernardo?" shouted Franz, as if coming out of a trance. "I'll kill him, as soon as I get my hands on him! This time he's gone too far."

Bernardo climbed over the side rail from outside the

glasshouse. "I've nothing to do with this!" he bellowed. "When are you going to get it through that pumpkin skull of yours," he said, knocking his hand against the side of Franz's head.

Before Franz could lunge at him, a voice said, "There'll be nobody killing anybody! One death is quite enough. That's all we'll hear of this talk. I'll not tolerate it at my glasshouse."

Master Webbe! Merry felt her knees buckle at the sight of him. He was wearing his cloak, the one he'd had on when he disappeared into the night. "Out of my way," he growled, pushing Merry aside. "I mean to get to the bottom of this. I'll not have this tomfoolery. Once was more than enough. Do you hear me? I'll not stand for it!" His boots crunched on the glass as he moved to inspect the damage.

Try as she might, Merry could not make sense of it. *He'll not get rich if he goes about destroying his own glass,* she thought. Perhaps he just drank too much and was in one of his tempers last night.

Master Webbe bent to the ground, studying something he'd found there among the broken pieces of glass. He picked it up and held it to the light. A blue glass bead.

"So 'tis you, Lupo," thundered Master Webbe. "I should have guessed. You're the only bead maker, and the only one to make glass of this color. 'Tis you who destroyed all my glass." Master Webbe nearly spat in Angelo's face. "I suspect 'twas you who tampered with the ovens as well!"

Angelo's face went ghost-white. "That's a lie," he said in a firm voice that shook with anger.

Master Webbe caught hold of the apprentice. He twisted Angelo's hands behind his back as if he were some kind of criminal. Then Master Webbe grabbed a handful of Angelo's shirt and dragged him away. "You'll hang for this, Lupo. I'll see to it myself."

The way Master Webbe shoved and pulled Angelo reminded Merry of her own horrible kidnapping. She couldn't stand it.

"He didn't do it!" Merry shouted in anger. "He didn't do anything! 'Tis the others are always fighting. And you, you're the one!" Merry shouted to Master Webbe. "You can't do this! Tell him, Franz!" she pleaded.

"Shhh!" said Franz. "You musn't make Master Webbe angry, else he'll drag you along also."

"Please, Franz, do something!" said Merry, tears streaming down her face. But all he did was hold her back from running after Master Webbe and Angelo.

"'Tis no use, Merry," said Franz. "Words will not bring back Angelo. 'Tis Bernardo who should be hauled off. I'm afraid nobody hears me when it comes to Bernardo. Master Webbe has made up his mind."

"Indeed he has," Bernardo sneered. "Look here." He held up Angelo's book. "Young Lupo seems to have left his book behind." Leafing through it, Bernardo said, "Ah.

'Tis all right here. I had such high hopes for him, but 'tis
clear that he has failed. Smashing the glass is simply proof
of his own frustration."

"Liar! Thief!" shouted Merry, reaching for the book.
"You stole that book. Give it to me!" Merry lunged, but
Franz held her back once more.

"Angelo is my apprentice," said Bernardo. "His work
belongs to me."

Franz nodded his head sadly in agreement.

"But what will happen to Angelo, Franz?" asked Merry.

"I'll stay here again tonight, until we catch the real
troublemaker. Then Angelo will haf his freedom."

"Where will they take him now?" asked Merry.

"Most likely into the town square," said Franz.

The town square . . . the stocks! They would put Angelo
in the stocks until the governor heard his case. Then he
would most likely be . . . Merry could hardly let herself
even think the word. *Hanged.*

"Master Webbe be cursed!" cried Merry, running from
the glasshouse.

"Merry, wait!" called Franz.

But she did not wait. She didn't care what ugly things
she'd said. All she cared to do was get as far away as possi-
ble. Merry fled, ablaze with an anger hot as molten glass.

CHAPTER 10

'TIS I

Merry ran. She ran as she'd run the day that horrible man had grabbed her on the streets of London, the day she'd been caught and thrown aboard that miserable ship. How she wished her feet could take her far away from this dreadful place called Jamestown.

Lies, all lies! How could this be happening? she thought.

Merry stood on the riverbank. She looked out on the river that led to the vast sea she'd crossed weeks ago. The sea that had taken her away from Margaret, yet brought her together with Angelo. He was the only person besides Franz who'd not treated her like the servant she was.

The only true friend.

Merry listened to the gentle lapping of the waves on the shore. She shut her eyes, trying to let the sound soothe her, calm her racing heart, the way it had in her days as a young girl along the Thames River in London.

When Margaret worked late into the night and was not
there to sing to Merry, tell her a story, or whisper a prayer,
all Merry had to do was close her eyes to hear the rhythm
of water lapping on the shore.

But now it was no use.

Merry could not think straight. She needed to talk
with someone, sort this out. But who? How she wished
she could go straight to Captain Norton. There was no
one else. Bernardo was part of the plan, and Franz thought
it was useless to try and do anything more for Angelo.

Merry watched a sea bird circle, hover, and land right
on the water. As she gazed out over the water, she thought
she saw a black dot on the horizon. Shielding her eyes, she
could just make out the faint outline of a ship silhouetted
against the sun.

Merry could not help but think of her own passage
and the thrill of sighting land after those many months.
Soon these passengers would arrive, as she had, so full of
fear and hope.

The ship would reach Jamestown by nightfall, and
would be headed back for England shortly. All Merry had
to do was wait for the right moment. She'd stow away on
that very ship until it set sail again.

But where would she go? Back to the streets of London?
As much as she missed Margaret, that was no life.

And she couldn't run away when Angelo was in danger
for his life. Angry as she was, she could not bear the

thought of deserting her friend.

Restless, Merry paced the shore, leaving footprints back and forth in the sand. There were several skiffs moored at the water's edge that the colonists used for getting around the inland waterways. Merry jumped in a skiff and began rowing up the twisting river. She rowed and rowed, with no idea where she was going. All that mattered was that she kept moving. She rowed up a tiny creek surrounded by marsh grass, overgrown with a tangle of trees and vines, until all she could hear was the call of a mockingbird.

Leaving the skiff behind, Merry climbed out onto the shore. Questions tumbled about like river rocks in Merry's mind. The stolen book, the tampering with the ovens, the death of Captain Norton, the smashed glass. And now Angelo. Was it all part of the same plot, and was Master Webbe behind it all? Why would he destroy the glasshouse, if that's where he and Bernardo planned to make *cristallo*? Merry tried to fit the pieces together in her mind. But try as she might, they only made a jumble.

She had to find a way to help Angelo. She pulled down a few grapevines from the tangle overhead, braiding them together to give her cold hands something to do as she tried to think of an idea that would prove her friend's innocence. Surely they couldn't hang him with one blue bead as the only evidence?

One blue bead. Merry wiped her chapped hands across

her apron and untied the cord of beads that Angelo had hung round her neck. She fingered each one of the beads, thinking of her friend's wide smile as he presented her with such a lovely token of friendship.

As the beads caught the sunlight, Merry realized that Angelo was right—the beads he'd made were not a perfect match to the beads her parents had given her. Angelo's beads were lighter in color; they reminded Merry of a blue jay's feather, or the shiny inside of a mussel shell. Merry thought of the quick-tempered Master Webbe's face as he lifted the bead from the glasshouse floor. But Merry now realized that the bead in Master Webbe's hand had been *deep* blue. The bead he had used to accuse Angelo was *her own*—the one she'd given Angelo for inspiration, the one he thought he had lost.

As quick as the glint of sun on a glass bead, the idea came to her. Merry wondered if she had the courage. She'd have to return to Jamestown right away. Already the December sky was clouding over, beginning to darken. And Merry had left, abandoned her friend when he was most likely locked in the stocks in the public square. She winced, thinking of people shouting ugly things at him and casting rotten vegetables and bad eggs, with no one there who would so much as wipe his face.

Merry jumped back in the skiff and rowed for home. Each pull of the oars set her muscles taut, stiffening her determination. A large osprey screeched in the oncoming darkness. She'd heard tales of flying squirrels, beasts that stretched their skins like kites to glide from tree to tree. She watched out for raccoons—masked phantoms that looked like monkeys—and strong-smelling muskrats, with heads of swine and tails of rats.

Merry rowed faster. Despite her aching arms, she rowed as if she might keep ahead of the last ruins of daylight. Now that she'd made up her mind, she could not return to Jamestown quickly enough.

As the dark deepened, Merry noticed something unusual. Each time she dipped her oar into the water and pulled it back, the water glowed with a greenish-white light. At first a spark, then a flicker, then nearly a clean ribbon of light. She peered over the side of the skiff, only to discover that her boat was surrounded with glowing, jellylike creatures. When she skimmed them with her oar, they lit up like a gather of glass being blown. Their warm glow comforted Merry as she glided silently back to the familiar shores of Jamestown, circled in a halo of light.

The ship Merry had seen earlier that day had since anchored at the wharf. The shores were abustle with confusion, people rushing here and there, talking and laughing and calling out to one another.

The ship has brought new servants to the colony, no doubt,

thought Merry. *And a boatload of tobacco brides.* Yesterday
the excitement might have been of great interest to her,
but the arrival of servants and wives, trading goods and
shipping supplies had little meaning to her now that her
friend's life was at stake.

Merry tied up the skiff and hurried up the rutted road
to the center of town, the same path she'd taken the day
of her arrival. Just outside the gates of the fort, she stopped
to remove a few of the original beads from her necklace
and slipped them into her right-hand pocket. Then she
purposefully tore a small hole in the empty pocket of her
apron.

Merry came to the center square, but the stocks were
empty. No crowds. No Angelo. A young servant about her
own age was picking through eggshells and chicken bones
on the ground, searching for food among the remnants
left by onlookers.

"Where is everyone? Has someone been in the stocks
today?" Merry asked him.

"The apprentice from the glasshouse, he was here.
Most o' these eggs were for him." The boy laughed.

"Do you know where they've taken him?"

"To the governor's house to hear his case."

Merry thanked the boy and hurried away. What if the
boy was right? Somehow she, Meredith Shipman, had to
gain audience to speak with Governor Yeardley himself!
Her knees weakened just thinking about it. But surely if

Merry could survive kidnapping, crossing an ocean, and the wrath of Master Webbe, she could survive speaking with the governor.

Before she lost courage, she swallowed and marched herself directly to the governor's house. It was only a house, a tall dwelling with windows, but it seemed to sneer at her with an ugly grimace. Before anyone could stop her, she opened the huge wooden door and burst into a room where Master Webbe stood stating the charges against Angelo.

The room was small and dimly lit with candles. The governor himself was seated at a long table in the center of the room. In the candlelight, his shadow danced in the rafters, looming large over the room. He had a pocked face, and Merry noticed both the plume in his hat and the sword at his side.

People were crowded onto benches lined before the table, and many whispered among the ranks in back. Master Webbe stood in front of the table, holding Angelo by the elbow. Angelo's hands were bound behind his back.

"Willful destruction of property!" roared Master Webbe, with angry gusto.

"'Tis I who smashed the glass!" Merry shouted for all to hear.

The room buzzed with exclamations.

"Oyez, oyez! Silence is commanded in the court, upon pain of punishment! All manner of persons with any plaint

to enter, draw near!" called one of the governor's men.
" 'Twill be two shillings due the court for disturbance of
the governor's peace."

"Please," begged Merry. All eyes were upon her now.
" 'Tis I . . ." she said, in a voice hardly stronger than a mouse.

"Merí! No!" cried Angelo, turning around to face her.

"Let all persons come forth, for they shall be heard.
God save the King!"

"Merí! Don't say so! You know 'tis not the truth!" cried
Angelo.

"Enough!" commanded the governor. "To whom shall I
attribute this outburst in my court?"

" 'Tis I, Meredith Shipman," said Merry, in a voice now
sure and true. "I did willfully smash the glass at the estab-
lishment run by Master Webbe at Glass House Pointe."

Master Webbe stared at Merry, speechless, as if he had
never seen her before.

"I can prove it," said Merry.

"What proof have you?" asked the governor.

"The bead you hold as evidence dropped from my
pocket." Merry stepped forward to show her pocket hole.

"This is nonsense!" roared Master Webbe. "Surely you
can't convict on evidence of a pocket hole." The crowd
laughed. "The girl is addled in the head."

" 'Tis not only the hole, but these beads I have here,"
said Merry, showing a handful of the original beads from
her necklace. "I am the owner of the glass bead that

Master Webbe found among the broken glass. If you com-
pare these with the bead you have for evidence, you'll find
they are the same."

"Rubbish!" cried Master Webbe.

But Merry knew she was not mistaken. "Venetian
glass," she continued. "From a necklace given me by my
parents when I lived in England. A bit darker and more
even in color, you'll see, than the sample beads made here
by Angelo Lupo. Any glassblower who knows his trade
will tell you the same. Surely Master Webbe himself can
identify such a match. Their likeness cannot be denied."

Governor Yeardley placed the bead from the glasshouse
on the table. With a trembling hand, Merry set one of
hers next to it. The very beads that would prove Angelo's
innocence would also prove her guilt.

"Master Webbe?" asked the governor.

"Identical," conceded Master Webbe.

"The truth is plain," said Merry. "You see, I was angry.
I was forced aboard a ship, brought here to be a servant
against my will. Surely you cannot think I enjoy being
treated like a slave, day in and day out?"

"Untie the young man," pronounced Governor
Yeardley. "He has been falsely accused. Angelo Lupo, you
are free to go. This court is dismissed." He stood to go,
but not before adding his final sentence: "Take the girl."

CHAPTER 11

IMPRISONED

Merry shivered in the dark cold of her prison. She'd been taken to a shed behind the storehouse, more damp and cramped than the ship's 'tween deck and filled with a frightening quiet. The room had a tiny lone window up high, out of Merry's reach, covered with a weathered board that had given way to December's winds.

There was no bed or cot, not even a stool to sit on. The floor was so heaped with straw that Merry thought they might as well have stuck her in a barn. The only thing in the room was a bucket of water with a ring of ice floating on top. Merry was uncertain whether this was meant for her to drink or whether it was a fire bucket. It didn't matter. She could not even find it in her to take a swallow.

In the pale moonlight of this December night, Merry could hardly see the outline of her own hand. She heard footsteps and called out to the man who'd brought her here. "Please, may I have a candle?"

"Certainly not," said the man from somewhere outside.

Merry did not think a candle was too much to ask. Perhaps they feared she'd be careless with it and the place would go up in flames. Alone and hungry, all Merry could think of was the punishment that awaited her. Would they tie her to a tree or dunk her in the river? Would she have to suffer lashes or be fined a sum of money she did not have?

What if they added years to her indenture! What if they forced her to work in the fields picking worms from tobacco leaves day in and day out? Or worse yet, banished her from the colony? She might be turned out into the wilderness like a wild animal, left to fend for herself.

Merry sank down in a heap on the stale, scratchy straw. Any number of bugs and other pests might be hidden in the straw. Just the thought of many-legged creatures crawling over her in the night made her shiver. She curled up inside her cloak and closed her eyes, hoping sleep would bring escape. How she wished for one thin coverlet! She could not keep away thoughts of the chest filled with quilts back at the Webbes' house. To think that just yesterday she had slept there in warmth and comfort. Even sleeping in the glasshouse loft where Franz had hidden would suit her just fine.

Merry remembered the times she'd felt so lonely aboard the *Flying Hart*. But at least on the ship there were other people always crowded around. Would anyone remember she was here? Think to bring her food? How long would they keep her locked up in this foul place?

The silence rang in Merry's ears. Her stomach ached with hunger. She coughed in the damp cold and drew her cloak tighter, like arms around her.

In the middle of the night, a terrific storm woke Merry. Rain thundered on the roof and beat with fury against the sides of the shed. Tree branches scratched the roof like the claws of wild animals. A ghostly wind whistled and moaned through the cracks between the boards, sending a chill down her back.

Merry thought the whole shed might blow down on top of her and crush her. She huddled in a corner with her head tucked between her knees, trying not to get soaked by the icy rain coming through the window and the cracks in the wall.

She must have dozed, because the next thing she knew, she heard a knocking from outside. The wind had died down, so this time it was not a tree branch.

"Merí," whispered a voice through a crack in the wall. Then she heard it again, louder. "Merí! Are you in there? Can you hear me? 'Tis Angelo."

"Angelo!" cried Merry.

"I'm sorry. 'Tis the first I could come, with the storm. It must have given you an awful fright."

"I'm fine," said Merry, making an effort to keep her voice from shaking.

"Are you sure?"

"Just cold. And hungry."

"They didn't give you anything to eat?"

"Just water. What I would do for a chunk of bread!"

"Fear not," said Angelo. "I'll be back. I'll bring you a blanket and something to eat."

"Please stay!"

"I musn't," said Angelo. "'Tis nearly light out and I can't be seen here. I'll return tonight, I promise. I can't bear thinking of you in there all by yourself instead of me. Why did you take the blame, Merí?"

"I knew the punishment for a young girl would not be as harsh as what they would do to you."

"You saved my life again, Merí Shipman, and I swear upon my life I'll do the same for you in return. I'll find a way to free you!"

"Wait!" Merry protested, but Angelo was gone.

She was alone again. Through a blur of tears, Merry memorized the four walls that held her prisoner. Before long, every crack, splinter, and spiderweb was like an old friend. She counted knotholes in the boards to take her mind off her hunger.

She and Margaret had been hungry many a time in London, and she'd learned one thing—it did no good to imagine food when her belly was empty. Margaret always made up games to keep their minds off the hollowness in their stomachs. "You can have anything you wish for your middle name," Margaret would tell her. And they would whisper in the dark, *Maria, Elizabeth, Rebecca* . . .

Merry was nearly done counting knots in the third wall when she heard the lock jiggle. A man brought bread and a mug of broth that smelled of fish heads. Merry half expected to see floating fish eyes staring up at her.

"Bang on the door when you're through, and I shall return for it," said the guard.

"How long will I stay here?" Merry asked.

"Until the governor has time to sentence you," the guard replied.

As soon as he'd gone, Merry ate greedily, never minding that the bread was stale, hard as a stone. She gulped the broth as if it were the finest porridge.

᯽

True to his word, Angelo returned that night. He had bundled a loaf of bread in a blanket, which, after several tries, he managed to toss through the window. He also brought Merry news.

"Much of the glasshouse blew over in the storm. But no one was hurt, and none of the ovens was destroyed."

"That's good news," said Merry.

"Master Webbe has called all of the builders in the colony to rebuild it. They say 'twill take but a few days' time, with all the men that have joined them."

"Was Franz there when the glasshouse went down?"

"He wasn't there, thanks be to God. Master Webbe bade him go home. There was no need for a guard, he said, when the mischief maker was locked in the colony's jail."

"Master Webbe is the only mischief maker," said Merry. "I saw him myself, sneaking out in the night. I followed him nearly to the glasshouse. I'm certain Master Webbe shattered all that glass himself, Angelo, and planted that bead so he could have you hanged!"

"And he may still be trying. My murder would not be explained away so easily as Captain Norton's," said Angelo. "Master Webbe accused me of tearing down the glasshouse myself, in an act of revenge. If it weren't for the builders assuring him 'twas just the wind, we would be now together inside this jail, no?"

"Stay clear of him, Angelo," Merry whispered through the wall just as it was time for Angelo to go.

❧

Merry lost track of time. She could scarcely tell day from night. The only interruptions—all she had to look forward to—were the delivery of bread and broth and Angelo's stolen visits. They had still not thought of a plan to free Merry.

The waiting was worse than the punishment itself. Why didn't they come for her? She began to fear the waiting would drive her mad. Merry took off her necklace and slipped a bead from the cord. She made up a game, to give her mind something to do. She closed her eyes, tossed the bead into the air, and tried to hear where it landed. Then, on hands and knees, she slowly searched for it. When at last she found it, she started again by tossing it in the air. And again. And again.

One morning as she played the game, she heard guns firing in Christmas celebration. Now she understood the waiting. The governor would not hand down her punishment until Christmastime had passed. Merry hummed a quiet carol to herself, but it made her feel even worse.

⚘

"Merry, I've heard that Master Webbe has spoken to the governor, and your sentence will be made known before the new year," Angelo whispered through the wall one evening.

"At last. My punishment."

"But you did nothing! It makes me so angry I could tear this place down with my own hands," Angelo whispered fiercely.

"I'd have you burn the place down if I weren't locked inside . . ." Merry's words trailed off. She looked at the piles of straw around her, and the fire bucket.

"Angelo?" Merry whispered. "Have you a flint and steel with you? I have an idea."

Something was wrong.

That evening, the guard did not come when he always did. If she had to wait until tomorrow, it might be too late.

Her heart leaped when finally a knock came on the door. But instead of the regular guard, a ruddy-faced, red-haired man entered.

"Why do you come here?" she asked more sharply than she meant to. "Where is the other man, the guard?"

"Is that how 'tis, then?" the man answered. Merry saw that he had her broth, as always. "I've come to bring your dinner, unless you'll not be wanting it."

"No, no. I've grown quite fond of it," Merry lied. The man gave her a sideways look, handed her the mug, then started to leave the shed.

"Shall I bang on the door as always?"

"Bang on the door?" he asked, puzzled.

"Yes, the guard always has me bang on the door when I'm through. Then he knows to come to get the mug."

"I'll listen for ye, then," said the man, and left, locking the door behind him.

Merry did not even stop to gulp down the soup. Instead, she bent over a small mound of straw. She took Angelo's flint and steel out of her pocket and began striking them together.

Sparks flew like small squibs, but the fireworks were

too small to catch. Merry leaned closer. She'd started a fire nearly every morning since she'd arrived at Jamestown, but this night not one spark wanted to catch. Perhaps it was the trembling of her hands. She stopped to listen, making certain no one was coming. Then she tried again.

At last, a tiny spark landed and caught. Merry blew on it gently, coaxing it along. The straw smoldered, smoked, then caught fire. She waited until flames licked along the ends of the straw. Then she blew on them some more.

The flames burst forth, nearly singeing the ends of her hair. She tossed the contents of the mug into the corner and banged on the door.

"Fire!" she shouted. "FIRRRRE!" She pounded against the door. Flames leaped and burst around her. Merry felt her heart rise in fear, a fear she hadn't expected.

What if no one came to her?

"Please! Help! Fire!" she called again, and this time she heard the lock rattle, and the man burst through the door.

"What the devil . . . ? Why didn't you douse it?" yelled the man. He set about stomping out the fire, then reached for the bucket of water.

That's when Merry raced out the door and into the cover of blackness. She ran through town, feet flying, faster than fire racing through straw.

CHAPTER 12

CAUGHT

M erry ran until her sharp breathing felt like flames inside her, and she had to stop to calm her pounding heart. She heard the fort's alarm bell ringing in the distance. The guard was alerting the town about the fire. Soon the whole colony would discover she'd escaped. They'd have to put out the fire before they could search for her, though. Was there a chance they would wait till daylight to search for her?

She and Angelo were both in danger now. The townspeople might suspect he had helped her escape. Despite the stabbing pains in her sides, she forced herself to run again until she reached the cover of trees just outside the glasshouse.

Merry inched closer, darting from tree to tree. She took two sticks from the woodpile and struck them together to get Angelo's attention.

"Who's there?" Angelo came outside at her signal,

looking carefully over each shoulder. Merry stepped out of the shadows. Angelo put a comforting arm around her and led her inside.

"I put aside some beans and bread to bring for you, and I've put warm blankets in the loft. I'll hide you there for now until we can think of what to do."

Merry wearily climbed the ladder to the loft. As she lay on the blankets, her muscles twitched with nervous exhaustion. Soon Angelo brought her a dish of beans he had warmed right in the glasshouse oven. Merry tore into the bread and gulped down the beans hungrily.

After she had finished, Angelo said, "I'll come at first light to wake you before the others arrive. We'll have to think of a better hiding place, until we come up with a sure way to show your innocence."

Merry nodded as her lids lowered, and she fell into a deep, exhausted sleep.

A crash startled Merry awake. Metal on metal. It sounded as if someone had dropped something in the dark or knocked over the glassmaking tools.

Merry sat bolt upright. Was she found out?

She stayed absolutely still. Even her soft breathing seemed too loud. She listened, and heard faint rustling and shuffling sounds below.

Crawling quietly on her stomach, Merry inched her way over to peek through a crack in the floorboards of the loft. She saw nothing but thick, black darkness. She wriggled closer, pressing her eye to the crack, and waited. A strand of her hair fell across her face. It tickled, but she didn't dare to blow it out of the way.

Then, the light of a single candle revealed the shadowy outline of a figure leaning over the back of the cooling oven. Merry squinted, trying to make out who the person was, but it was too dim to tell. The man was removing clay and rubble from the drafts in back of the oven. He held something in his hand, as if he meant to toss whatever it was through the working hole into the oven. He moved his arm in a circle, binding or wrapping something. Then he stood, his back to Merry.

The man's shadow loomed large on the ceiling. He wore a long cape, and when he moved his arm in a circle again and spread the cape, the light shone through a jagged tear.

Master Webbe.

But what was he doing? He had something strung over his shoulder. Several things, all hanging at his side. In the flickering light, Merry could see him binding them together. As he turned to the light, Merry saw what they were.

Powder flasks!

She took in a sharp breath. Could he possibly mean to toss gunpowder into the oven flames? Merry could not believe it. The gunpowder would explode with enough of a blast to tear the roof off the whole place!

Merry felt as if she might choke. She had to do something before she was blown sky-high right along with the glasshouse.

"*Stop at once!*" Merry shouted. The figure below her looked up.

Merry scrambled down the ladder from the loft and stood face to face with the intruder. But now she could see that it wasn't the scar-faced Master Webbe. The intruder she stared at wasn't a man at all.

'Twas Mistress Webbe in her husband's clothing!

Merry stood stone still, in shock.

"Merry! What are you doing here?" Mistress Webbe spat out.

" 'Twas you!" Merry shouted in disbelief. "You tampered with the ovens and smashed the glass!" And she and Angelo had nearly paid for it with their lives. Merry boiled with anger.

"Please, Merry," Mistress Webbe said. Her voice took on a coaxing tone. "We can help each other. Just listen to me. If you keep quiet about what you have seen here tonight, I myself will attest to your innocence. I promise to take you back to England with us."

"But I am guilty of nothing!" protested Merry. "I do not wish to return to England, and I will not go anywhere with you. You put my friend's life in danger, and now my own!"

Mistress Webbe grabbed Merry by the shoulders. "Merry, you must think clearly. You are only a servant girl. I am the respected wife of a merchant who runs the glasshouse. Just think what the governor will say when I tell him I've caught you. Everyone already believes you're responsible for all the devilment here. 'Twill not be difficult to imagine yet another crime. You escaped in the night and made haste for the glasshouse for your final revenge."

Merry struggled to break loose.

"'Tis the only way for us both to escape punishment," Mistress Webbe said, narrowing her eyes at Merry.

At last, Merry wrenched herself from Mistress Webbe's grip. She raced for the alarm bell and pulled the cord again and again. The bell's ringing pierced the night.

Mistress Webbe fled like a rat caught eating stores of corn. The glassmakers came running. Angelo shouldered his way through. "Merí, are you in danger?" he cried.

Before Merry could answer, Franz arrived, holding Mistress Webbe by the arm. She still wore the powder flasks around her neck, and gunpowder had spilled down the front of Master Webbe's cloak.

"Franz!" Merry shouted. "She meant to blow up the glasshouse!"

"I didn't mean harm to anyone!" cried Mistress Webbe. "You must believe me!"

Just then Master Webbe arrived. He looked around in angry bewilderment, swelling like a toadfish nearly ready to burst at what he saw—gunpowder strewn about, glass-makers huddled in the middle of the night, and Mistress Webbe, his own wife, dressed in his cloak and boots, dirt-streaked and tearful.

Mistress Webbe threw herself at him and sobbed.

"What nonsense is this, woman?" growled Master Webbe. "I do not see—"

"You do not see! You do not hear!" she exclaimed. "You're the one who drove me to this! You forced me to live in this contemptible wilderness, with cold and fever and every manner of wild beast! Pigs roam the streets, for heaven's sake. The entrails of the earth, this place is. You refused to see how miserable I've been from the first."

"What is this all about?" asked Master Webbe.

"Your wife meant to send up the ovens this night, sir," said Merry. She pointed to the powder flasks. "She wanted to explode the place to pieces."

"What!" Master Webbe shouted. He turned to his wife. "Surely this isn't true?"

"'Tis the truth!" she said. "And I am not ashamed for you to hear it. At long last you will listen. Can't you under-stand?" asked Mistress Webbe, holding her face in her hands. "I thought if I could see to it that the glasshouse failed, you would finally take me back to England.

"'Twas you who gave me the idea," she continued. "One night, I overheard you and Bernardo talking about *cristallo*. You talked of how you might steal the formula from young Lupo and make yourselves wealthy."

"Nonsense!" spat Master Webbe, not meeting eyes with Angelo.

"'Tis true!" Merry exclaimed. "I heard them my first night here and warned Angelo the very next morning." Angelo nodded in agreement. Bernardo simply fixed his eyes on the ground.

"So you tampered with our ovens," Franz said in astonishment.

"Yes, my years as a glasshouse wife finally served me well. I knew exactly how to keep you from making glass. And when you did succeed in making some, I smashed it." A murmur of disbelief rippled through the crowd of glassmakers.

"With the young apprentice getting nearer and nearer to *cristallo,* I knew we'd never leave. As long as there were riches to be made, I knew my husband would do anything to stay—maybe even murder Captain Norton!" Mistress Webbe shot out, turning on her husband.

Master Webbe looked up in utter shock. The color drained from his face, until he appeared ghostly in the candlelight. But he didn't breathe a word, as if all the air had gone right out of him.

CHAPTER 13

MERRY!

The next day, Merry found herself standing once more in front of the governor. But this time, her knees did not quake.

She tried to follow what was happening, amid all the confusing words and people and questions and shouts of "God save the King!" Mistress Webbe stood trial before the governor and his court of justices. Master Webbe stood next to her. Witnesses were brought forth, and Merry herself was called on to repeat the story of last night's activities. Whisperings grew louder as the colonists heard her tale.

"Silence is commanded in the court while His Majesty's justices are sitting, upon pain of punishment," said a man in a long coat and vest.

A clerk read the charges, stating that Mistress Webbe did knowingly and evilly attempt to destroy the glasshouse, with considerable risk to life and limb.

When all was said and done, the governor declared,
"Mistress Elizabeth Webbe, the court finds you guilty as
charged. You are to be banished from the colony of Virginia.
'Tis so ordered by this court, under protection of the Crown,
punishment to be effective immediately."

Master Webbe fiercely denied that he had stolen
Angelo's book or murdered Captain Norton. There was
no way to prove otherwise. All accusations were dropped.
But Merry soon learned that if a wife commits a crime,
the husband, too, is held liable. So Master Webbe was pun-
ished for the wrongdoings of Mistress Webbe.

They were both to be shipped off to a plantation
called Bermuda Hundred, a neck of land far to the north,
destined for manual labor in the fields. The governor
ordered that the Webbes' house and all of their property
be turned over to the colony.

As for Bernardo, hurt pride and failure to discover a
new formula for *cristallo* seemed punishment enough. He
would sail back to England in shame, never to return to
Italy or Jamestown again.

What will become of me, Merry wondered, *with the
Webbes gone and Captain Norton dead?*

Then came Merry's turn before the governor. He
spoke to her solemnly. "Let it be known that the court
hereby pardons Meredith Shipman. On behalf of the
colony of Virginia, I declare Meredith Shipman free and
clear of her indenture, her contract no longer binding.

'Tis with deep regard for the courage and fortitude she has shown that I, in the name of the colony, present her this day with her Certificate of Freedom."

Merry held the certificate in front of her, tracing the letters of her own name. She felt as if her feet would no longer stay on the ground, as if she had grown wings.

Angelo and Franz each hugged her in turn and gazed at the certificate.

"You are free, Merí," said Angelo. "Free! No one is more deserving."

"Because of you, this devilment is ended," said Franz. "Without you, we would no longer haf a glasshouse."

Merry held in her two hands the proof of her freedom. She could hardly take her eyes off of it.

≪≫

When they returned to the glasshouse, Franz took Merry aside. "Of course I can give you nothing that compares with a gift of freedom, but please allow me to give you a more humble gift," said Franz. He handed Merry a delicate, slim-necked bottle of fern-green glass with his special seal on the front bearing the initials *MS*.

"Thank you," Merry said softly. Her eyes brimmed with tears. "Please, Franz, may I be excused for a short while?" At his nod, she set the bottle down and hurried from the glasshouse down to the river's edge.

She breathed in the salty smell of the water, letting the cold air fill her. *I'm free!* she thought. *Free!*

Walking along the water's edge, she remembered gathering shells that first day, when the glasshouse had seemed so strange, so new. Somehow, it had become home to her, full of people who trusted her and cared about her—a place where she mattered. Merry made footprints in the sand going one direction, then stepped within those same prints on the way back, deep in thought.

As Merry returned to the glasshouse, she began to worry. *I am free now,* she thought, *but where will I go?*

"There you are, Merí," said Angelo, walking down the path to meet her. "Mistress Norton is here. She'd like to speak with you."

"Mistress Norton?"

"Yes," said Angelo. "Now that Captain Norton has passed on, the widow Norton is in charge until all his matters are settled. She hopes to inherit the glasshouse and has decided that Franz will be put in charge of it, in place of Master Webbe."

"That's wonderful news!" said Merry, as they walked along the path.

When they entered the glasshouse, Mistress Norton called out, "Merry, come here, my dear girl." She took Merry's hand and pressed it between both of hers. "I came to thank you for saving the glasshouse, but now that I see you face to face, no words seem enough thanks for all you've done for us. 'Tis not every day that we have a girl who catches a criminal in our midst."

Merry beamed.

"I trust you'll be staying on at Jamestown?" asked Mistress Norton.

"I hope 'tis not too bold of me to ask, Mistress Norton, but I'd like to know if there's any hope of keeping me on at the glasshouse. I'm a hard worker, and I can learn to measure and mix ingredients."

Mistress Norton looked at Franz. "Why, I think that's a fine idea, if Franz agrees to it."

"I'm happy to haf you, Merry," said Franz. "I'll need some good hands to prepare the glass. Angelo is to become a glassblower in his own right."

"Angelo!" cried Merry. "You didn't breathe a word!"

"I just found out myself!" exclaimed Angelo.

There were laughs and handshakes all around.

"Mistress Norton has asked us to report to Mr. Leak," Franz told Angelo, "to bring him news that his glass will be finished once and for all."

"The poor man must be wondering if he will ever see the glassware for his new bride," said Mistress Norton. "Perhaps you'd like to go with Angelo," Mistress Norton said to Merry. "If 'tis all right with Franz."

"Ya, that would be quite a good idea," said Franz.

When Merry arrived with Angelo at Mr. Charles Leak's plantation, she met the planter for the first time. Merry could not help liking him from the start, with his friendly, dark brown eyes and welcoming smile.

"Merry, is it?" asked the man, giving her a warm handshake. "Word travels fast in the colony. We've heard a great deal about you, miss, these last few days," he said. "I daresay my bride-to-be is most eager to see you."

"She has arrived, then?" asked Merry.

"Aboard the *Warwick*," said Mr. Leak. "She arrived at dusk many days ago, in time for the new year. We are to be wed on Twelfth Night. Two years I've waited for this day!"

Merry remembered the ship she'd noticed the night she'd seen the jellyfish—the night she'd been locked in the shed behind the storehouse.

"We've had much to preoccupy us at the glasshouse these last days, no?" said Angelo.

While Angelo told Mr. Leak of the problems at the glasshouse and the present state of his order, Merry gazed around the room. The walls were snowy white, and curtains hung at the windows. The room was filled with real English furniture and even had a brick chimney! Through the window, beyond the tobacco barns, Merry saw tilled fields ready and waiting.

"We'll be planting tobacco this January," said Mr. Leak, taking note of Merry's interest. "What do you think of the place we have here?"

"Oh, 'tis fine!" said Merry. "I haven't seen such lovely things since I left London."

At that, Mr. Leak laughed. "I can't say that my friends in London would consider it fine, but I do hope it suits my bride. She's cost me a pretty penny," he teased, pointing to the goods that lay across the table. Merry feasted her eyes on a dress, a waistcoat, gloves, a hat, stockings, a petticoat, and more.

"Best hang on to that necklace," said Mr. Leak, "or she just may fancy it for herself. She has quite an interest in beads, this girl."

"Where is she?" asked Merry.

"Forgive me if I have seemed rude." In walked a young woman in a silken dress that matched her eyes, the color of the first green of the willow. Around her neck was a simple cord of dark blue beads. "I only wanted to make my entrance at the proper time." Her voice reached Merry's ears like a song from childhood.

"Margaret!" cried Merry, rushing over to her and throwing her arms around her sister. "How can this be? Tell me my eyes do not play me a cruel trick!"

Margaret laughed and replied, "Your eyes do not deceive you." Then her brow creased with concern.

"Oh, Merry, it has been awful. I couldn't bear the thought of you being locked up, and they refused to tell me where you'd been taken! No one believed I was your sister. I tried to see the governor and was tossed out like a head of cabbage. Then we heard you had escaped, and I was sick with worry. I couldn't think what to do but make arrangements at the glasshouse in hopes that as soon as you were found they would notify me."

"'Tis over now. You're here, Margaret Shipman!" exclaimed Merry as she hugged her sister all over again. She could hardly believe Margaret was standing right before her, here in Jamestown.

Margaret held her tightly, then smiled widely. "Soon, my dear," she said, "you must grow accustomed to calling me Margaret Leak!"

Twelve days after Christmas, on the eve of Twelfth Night, Mr. Leak hosted a glorious wedding celebration. Friends and family, new and old, gathered around a bonfire to feast, sing, and dance. Everyone Merry loved and cared about surrounded her, except for one person.

Where was Angelo?

At last, he appeared in the ring of firelight and came over to Merry. He was out of breath, and held out a small wooden box wrapped with a dark red ribbon.

"Is this a wedding gift for Margaret?" Merry asked.

"No, 'tis for you. Open it," said Angelo with a smile.

Amid the noise and merriment and firecrackers, Merry carefully untied the ribbon and slowly lifted the lid.

There, on a silken cord, lay a single beautiful bead—a bead of clear glass, pure and sparkling as a droplet of ice.

"Cristallo!" exclaimed Merry with joy as she held it to the light. Merry could see straight through that clean glass. She hugged Angelo tight. "I knew it wasn't just an accident. I knew you could do it!"

Merry was thrilled for Angelo, and for the glasshouse, but she knew no gift could ever be as great as those she'd been given these last days—a real home with her sister Margaret, the kindness and generosity of true friends, work that kept her busy and happy. And most cherished of all, her freedom.

Merry could scarcely believe that Margaret had found her, let alone that she was now married. Margaret, her own sister, a tobacco bride! In the days since her arrival, Margaret had told the whole story several times. But Merry pleaded to hear it once again.

" 'Twas the dock boy, John Stone, who came to the Sign of the Swan with word of your kidnapping. For a hunk of warm bread, he told me that Jamestown was where they were taking you. I asked everyone about this place called Jamestown. I was told all manner of riches lay in the New World. Why, the wife of the tavern keeper spoke of a cousin who had sailed as a tobacco bride on the *Bona Nova* a year ago—her passage paid and a husband found!

"All I had to do was provide a letter to a ship's captain attesting to my honesty and virtue, and prove I had a useful skill. Though my embroidery is sorely lacking, I was told I had skills that were wanted here as a planter's wife, in baking, butter-churning, and cheese-making. And for that, I would gain a husband and a brand-new life!"

"And a lost-and-found sister!" said Merry.

Margaret hugged Merry close.

"Who would have thought," Margaret continued, "that I'd arrive to find my own sister locked up that very day. Even Charles could not gain me admittance. Until the day I found out you were free, I thought I might never see you again! But here you are, standing before me, as certain as this ring on my finger."

The whole crowd cheered and raised their glasses to Merry and Margaret.

"We must all have cake," exclaimed Margaret, her face glowing. "We've a Twelfth cake, in honor of our wedding. A coin is baked inside this cake, and whoever finds it is assured good luck for the coming year."

Margaret and Mr. Leak cut the cake and passed slices all around. Merry tried a few tender bites, chewing carefully. Suddenly, her teeth came down on something hard.

She pulled a small shiny object from her mouth. "The coin!" she called out. "I've found it!"

"'Tis Merry who shall have good luck upon her in the coming year!" cried Margaret.

"It has already begun," said Merry, "with all of you."

A PEEK INTO
THE PAST

THE
NEW LIFE
of Virginea:
DECLARING THE
FORMER SVCCESSE AND PRE-
sent estate of that plantation, being the second
part of *Noua Britannia.*

Published by the authoritie of his Maiesties
Counsell of *Virginea.*

LONDON,
Imprinted by *Felix Kyngston* for *William Welby,* dwelling at the
signe of the Swan in Pauls Churchyard. 1612.

LOOKING BACK: 1621

On May 13, 1607, three overcrowded ships—Godspeed, Susan Constant, and Discovery—brought the first English settlers to the shores of Virginia.

At the time of Merry's story, England was in fierce competition with Spain, which had a powerful *armada,* or fleet of warships, and prospering colonies in the New World. Spain's colonies gave its ships safe harbor as they sailed the world in search of riches. In 1606, a group of Englishmen formed the Virginia Company of London and sent 104 men and boys across the Atlantic Ocean to form the first permanent English colony in America. They hoped to find gold and silver, as the Spanish had to the south, and also raw materials to help fuel England's industries.

America in 1606
- British Territory
- Spanish Territory
- French Territory
- Uncharted

After four months at sea, the settlers landed on Virginia's coast and then sailed up the James River until they found a place they called Jamestown Island. It was actually a peninsula surrounded by water on three sides, where they could anchor easily and defend themselves against attacks from the Spanish or the Indians.

Unfortunately, they couldn't have picked a worse spot to settle. Instead of gold, they found a swampland full of mosquitoes, snakes, and frogs. On top of that, most of the settlers were gentlemen who didn't know a thing about farming or hunting. Some wore 60-pound suits of metal armor to protect themselves while hunting. The clanking scared away all the game!

The colonists *did* manage to send some valuable raw materials to England, such as tar and pitch, and they tried to make goods the Virginia Company could sell in England. Bricks, boats, wine, and glass were among these early "tryalls." The demand for glass in England was great, yet few Englishmen were skilled in the craft.

In 1608, the Virginia Company sent skilled German and Polish glassmakers to Jamestown. They built a glasshouse one mile from Jamestown on a narrow bridge of land known as

"Common green" was the easiest glass color to make with Jamestown's materials.

Glass House Pointe. To make glass, they gathered wood and burned it, then leached the ashes to make *potash,* a source of potassium. They mixed potash with sand, added *cullet,* or broken glass, and heated these ingredients over intense fire until they turned to a liquid ready to be blown into glass.

The colonists' industries never got off the ground. Their food supply had dwindled so low that the years 1609–1610 were known as the Starving Time. The colonists hadn't managed to plant any crops, and they'd made enemies of the local Indians, who refused to trade with them for food. Of the 500 people in Jamestown by that time, only 60 survived.

In June of 1610, the survivors decided to try to sail back to England. They said good-bye to Jamestown forever. Or so they thought. No sooner had they set sail for England than they passed an incoming ship bringing supplies and 300 more settlers. Jamestown was given a second chance.

Settlers ate dogs, cats, rats, snakes, and even shoes during the Starving Time. Here, a man deals out five kernels of corn to each settler.

One of the new settlers was a man named John Rolfe, who discovered a special tobacco leaf that grew easily in Jamestown's swampy land. Tobacco was highly prized in England. At last, Jamestown had found its gold. Colonists began growing the "golden weed" everywhere—they even planted it in the streets!

Despite the money the Virginia Company made from tobacco, it was still deeply in debt from the colony's early struggles. Company members tried everything they could think of to lure people to the

King James warned that tobacco smoke was "hateful to the nose, harmful to the brain, and dangerous to the lungs." Still, the English smoked with gusto and believed tobacco could cure headaches and kill fleas.

New World. They gave more land to their investors so they could grow even more tobacco. Many of the investors in England sent *indentured servants* to Jamestown to grow tobacco for them. Indentured servants signed a contract that said they would work for a master for four to seven years. In exchange, the master paid their passage to the New World and provided room and board. When the contract was fulfilled, the servant was free.

In 1619, the Virginia Company established the *headright system*. If a person paid his own way to the colony, the company gave him 50 acres of land, and 50 more acres for every person whose passage he paid. Ship captains were often hired to recruit people to come to Jamestown. Some poor people came willingly as indentured servants, hoping for a better life. Others were criminals who were offered indentured servitude as a way to work off their prison sentences. Still others were kidnapped, as Merry is in the story.

Advertisements boasted of great opportunity for wealth in the New World.

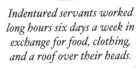

Indentured servants worked long hours six days a week in exchange for food, clothing, and a roof over their heads.

The tobacco industry became so successful that many tobacco planters decided to stay in Jamestown permanently. They had land, homes, and money, but they were missing one thing: wives. The Virginia Company began advertising for women who wanted to become "tobacco brides." Ships carrying young "maides" began arriving in Jamestown in 1620. They received petticoats, stockings, garters, gloves, hats, aprons, shoes, towels, sheets, rugs . . . and a husband!

At last, the colony was firmly on its feet. In August of 1621, the year Merry arrives at Jamestown, the colonists again tried glassblowing. Captain Norton was a real person who came to Jamestown

For 120 pounds of tobacco, a planter could buy himself a bride.

with the dream of becoming rich through glassmaking. He convinced six Italian glassblowers, men like the fictional Bernardo and Angelo, to join him. Captain Norton hoped to make *cristallo,* a highly desirable clear glass that had been crafted only in Italy. At the time, Italian glassblowers were forbidden to share the secret formula. Men like Angelo and Bernardo would have been smuggled out of Italy, never to return to their homeland.

In the mystery, one kind of trouble after another takes place at the glasshouse. This was true in history, too. There was fierce competition between the German and the Italian glassblowers,

A cristallo *vase made in Florence, Italy, in 1618*

which caused a lot of fighting and bickering. Many of the Italian glassblowers fell ill from malaria and yellow fever, and Captain Norton himself met an untimely death. And the whole glasshouse blew down in a fierce storm, just as Angelo reports to Merry when she is locked in jail.

Today, most glass is made by machine, but some artists still keep the magic of glassblowing alive. They learn to blow glass the same way Angelo did, and use many of the same tools. The handblown perfume bottles, pitchers, drinking glasses, and necklace beads you see in stores today are much the same as those Merry helped make in 1621.

Above: Glassblowers still make traditional glass at Jamestown today.
At left: Modern blown glass comes in every shape and color imaginable.

AUTHOR'S NOTE

Special glass bottles with a seal bearing the owner's family crest or initials, like the one Franz gives to Merry, really did exist, but probably not until 1667. I included those bottles in Merry's story because as an orphan and an indentured servant, seeing her own initials on something would have meant a lot to Merry, and I wanted her to receive such a distinctive gift of honor in 1621.

ABOUT THE AUTHOR

Megan McDonald grew up in a house stuffed with books (and older sisters!) in Pittsburgh. Her first job after college took her to Colonial National Historical Park in Jamestown. As a park ranger, she conducted tours of Jamestown Island, where she first learned about the working glasshouse at Glass House Pointe. She has written many books for children, including *Insects Are My Life* and *Judy Moody*. She and her husband live in Sebastopol, a small town in northern California.

FREE CATALOGUE!

American Girl Gear is all about who you are today—smart, spirited, and ready for anything! Our catalogue is full of clothes and accessories that let you express yourself, with great styles for every occasion!

For your **free** catalogue, return this postcard, call **1-800-845-0005**, or visit our Web site at **www.americangirl.com**.

Send me a catalogue:

_____
My name

_____
My address

_____
City   State   Zip 12567

My birth date: _____/_____/_____
               month day year

Send my friend a catalogue:

_____
My friend's name

_____
Address

_____
City   State   Zip 12575

_____
My e-mail address

_____
Parent's signature

Subscribe today to *American Girl* – the magazine written especially for you!

For just $19.95, we'll send you 6 big bimonthly issues of **American Girl.** You'll get even more games, giggles, crafts, projects, and helpful advice. Plus, every issue is jam-packed with great stories about girls just like you!

Yes! I want to order a subscription.
❑ Bill me ❑ Payment enclosed

Send bill to: (please print)

_____
Adult's name

_____
Address

_____
City   State   Zip

Send magazine to: (please print)

_____
Girl's name

_____
Address

_____
City   State   Zip

Girl's birth date: _____/_____/_____
                   month day year

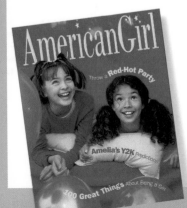